The Crimson Child

By R.N. Morris

First published in 2023 by Sharpe Books.

1

Spring. 1880.

It was General Krolikov's name day, the day he celebrated being Timofei son of Timofei.

He chose to spend it in Tavrichesky Garden, St Petersburg, as he did every year, weather permitting. As usual, his daughter Vera had arranged a party. Most of those in the group were strangers to him. He assumed they were members of his family. Nephews and nieces who had grown up in his absence. Distant cousins and their interchangeable offspring. And now there was a whole gaggle of brats running around his legs. Someone had even brought along a yapping dog, one of those awful miniature lapdogs. He wouldn't mind if it was a proper hound.

He only ever saw his relatives on his name day. And between one year and the next, he forgot all their names.

Why were they here? What did they want from him? They brought him gifts he didn't want. What did they expect from him in return?

No doubt they thought he was rich, because of his connections at court and his years of colonial service. No one came back from the Caucasus poor, no one sensible did.

Well, maybe he was rich, but they weren't getting their grubby hands on any of his fortune.

He hated the way they simpered and fawned. Was that why his name day always put him in a bad mood? They smiled like imbeciles. No, it was worse than that. They smiled as if *he* were the imbecile. And he knew what they wanted. They wanted him to remember them, to say their names without prompting.

Because then there was a chance that he would remember them in his will.

Krolikov smiled to himself. *Fat chance of that!*

There were picnic baskets and bottles of champagne. One of the advantages of growing old was that he didn't have to lug anything. The nameless relatives vied with each other to carry the heaviest

1

burden, making sure that he saw them. *See, uncle!* their faces beamed. More fool them. He didn't ask them to. Why not leave it to the servants?

But when he looked around, he couldn't see any servants.

'Where is Grigory?' he growled.

Vera was at his side. 'Grigory? Don't you remember, father? We talked about this?'

'Talked about what?'

'I gave all the servants the day off.'

'All of them? Why on earth did you do that?'

'Because we have no need of them. The boys can carry everything.'

'You shouldn't have done it without consulting me.'

'But I did consult you, father. You agreed.'

'No. I would never agree to it.'

'Well, you did.'

Krolikov lapsed into a reflective silence. Perhaps he did remember something about it now.

'Who are these people?'

'They are all the people who love you, father.'

'Jesus Christ.'

He noticed Vera watching him solicitously.

'But where are my friends?'

'We are your friends.'

'No, my real friends. Dmitri Petrovich, Alexei Andreevich, Boris Borisovich.' Krolikov looked about him, growing suddenly agitated. 'They are not here. And where are my brothers, Mikhail Timofeevich and Pavel Timofeevich?'

There was a beat before Vera replied: 'They are all dead, father.'

He winced at the brutality of her statement, wanted to punish her for her cruelty with a reprimand. 'Why didn't you invite the Emperor?' he demanded sharply.

'I did, father. He sent his apologies.' Vera looked away from her father and muttered under breath: 'As he does every year.'

'What about the Empress?'

'The Empress is very ill. They say she is dying.'

He came to a sudden stop on the path that led between an avenue of English oak trees. The whole park was laid out in the English style.

The party carried on without him. So that was how much they cared about him. They didn't even notice when he wasn't there among them. Even Vera had walked on a few paces. But at least she stopped as soon as she noticed he was no longer by her side.

She looked back at him with an expression of mute appeal.

He waved her on with a bad-tempered flick of his cane. 'I just want a moment to myself. Is that too much to ask? On my name day?'

Vera's look was now one of hurt, which quickly changed to disappointment. She turned her back on her father and hurried to catch up with her husband and her own daughter, who were in amongst the other relatives.

The day was fine but chilly. Although winter was behind them, the party had come out in overcoats and scarves. Krolikov felt the ice still there deep in his bones. The sun glinted unreliably through the gently swaying leaves, coming and going like an elusive memory.

There was a rustle of branches, and the place felt suddenly alien to him. Perhaps it was the unfamiliar foreign plants coming into bloom, or the subtle eccentricities of the landscape. But as he stood there an odd feeling came over him. He wondered where he was and how he had got there.

At that moment, from somewhere to his left, a peal of laughter reached him. It was light, musical, a young girl's laughter. A child mocking him? One of his confounded great nieces perhaps.

He turned in the direction of the sound and saw a girl of around eight or nine standing between two trees. She was dressed as a Circassian bride. Her silken bodice and skirt glinted a deep crimson, braided with gold. The domed headwear made her look like a strange and poisonous mushroom.

The girl stared directly at him, her eyes twinkling with impish mischief. She held her arms out to the sides, trailing a pair of long, loose sleeves like fairy wings.

As soon as he looked at her, she spun round, so that the veil that hung from the back of her headdress fanned out like a net cast into

3

the air. Then, skipping away deeper into the wooded area, she was gone. But even in the second that he had seen her, he knew.

He knew that it was *her*.

It was a little strange, he had to admit, that she was still a child. It was so many years ago now since he had last seen her. And yet, at the same time, it felt like it was only yesterday. But he was certain that it was her, the little minx. He would recognise those eyes anywhere.

More and more these days, Krolikov felt himself living in the past and the present simultaneously. As for the future, it interested him less and less, although others still tried to draw him into it.

At first it had frightened him, this slippage in time. But he had now reached a point where he welcomed it. Often, he experienced this living past as a pleasant dream. Or at least, that was how it always started. The years fell from him and he was young again.

There had been times, however, when the dream turned out to be not so pleasant. It would start innocuously enough, teasing him in with some tantalising vision of an old, long dead comrade. But then it would quietly and without warning unleash a vision of horror, or shame, or perhaps a combination of both, because the worst horrors were those for which he was to blame.

And so always there was a sense of foreboding as he felt the dream approach. Where would it take him this time?

Krolikov heard her tinkling laughter recede behind a screen of trees and stepped off the path to follow it.

He quickened his step into a headlong lurch, using his cane to keep his balance on the rougher ground. Massive roots snared his staggering feet. Hanging branches scratched his face. The lower, thicker boughs blocked him, so that he had to duck beneath them, or find another way through.

From time to time, he lost the trail. He would stand and listen, then catch sight of a flash of crimson and head off after it.

She led him into a small clearing, enclosed by a ring of trees whose sprawling branches meshed together overhead to form a dense canopy. It was a dark place, sunless and chill. What light there was, came refracted through leaves. It flickered in the air and fell lifeless on the dappled ground.

THE CRIMSON CHILD

In the centre of the clearing, with its back to Krolikov, there stood - Krolikov couldn't say with certainty what it was, but it seemed to be a figure formed from shadows condensed into human form.

He - for the figure seemed to be male - was wearing a long black coat which went almost to the ground, and a top hat decorated with black crape as if in mourning. The man, or possibly youth, was shorter than Krolikov. The general was in his seventies but despite his age, still presented a fine, tall figure, always standing straight and high with a proud, military bearing.

On the ground to one side of the mysterious youth lay a carpet bag. Krolikov immediately conceived an irrational dread of what the bag contained.

The girl had taken up a position on the other side, facing Krolikov. She giggled, a little nervously, he thought, before dancing off towards the edge of the clearing.

The figure began to turn slowly towards him.

This was the moment in the dream when the horror would be revealed.

And so it was. A pleasant, youthful face now confronted him, handsome, almost feminine. But the pleasing impression of the face was spoilt by its expression of wry mockery.

And the youth was holding a sword out in front of him.

Eyes locked on Krolikov's, the sinister figure began to spin the sword. The air sang as it was whipped by steel. The blade fractured into multiple ghostly images of itself. The youth's hand hardly moved, but the sword swirled in ceaseless motion.

The last time he had seen such swordsmanship was in the Caucasus. His men captured one of the mountain dwellers, who put on a defiant display for them.

Krolikov was rooted to the spot, mesmerised. Where would the dream end this time?

The youth took three brisk steps towards him. The sword's rapid swirling did not falter. The air sucked in its breath one final time.

Krolikov watched the blade's relentless swoop. By the time he realised it was aimed at him, it was too late.

There was another glassy tinkle of laughter. Then nothing.

2

Pavel Pavlovich Virginsky, investigating magistrate of the Rozhdestvenskaya District of St Petersburg, looked down at the headless body.

The air was shrill with birdsong. Of course the birds would keep on singing. It was not in their nature to stop, not even for this. He felt a sudden twitch of his upper lip as he suppressed a frivolous thought. The birds were all witnesses.

He was becoming hysterical, clearly. He needed to get a grip.

But this was too much. He was not ready for it. He couldn't cope with it. Not just with the horror of the crime, but with the sense of expectation directed towards him. It came from the uniformed police officers and detectives who were milling around the mutilated corpse, waiting for him to take charge of the investigation and issue clear and decisive orders. It came too from the higher-ups who had gathered around the body, drawn by the atrocity of the crime and the rank of the victim. But most of all it came from the dead man's family, who were at this moment being held in another part of the gardens, waiting for Virginsky to speak to them.

They were all looking to him to make sense of this. But how could anyone make sense of an old man cut down in this unspeakable manner?

'Where is it?' The question came out almost involuntarily. It was more that Virginsky was thinking aloud than that he expected an answer.

Sergeant Petrov stepped forward to provide an answer. 'The head, you mean? We haven't recovered it yet, your Honour.'

Virginsky allowed a moue of dissatisfaction to contort his lips. He did not doubt that Petrov was an adequate police officer, but he was no Sergeant Ptitsyn, whom Virginsky had worked with at the Stolyarny Lane station. Then Virginsky had been seconded to the Fontanka Embankment headquarters of the Third Section - the Tsar's secret police - on the orders of Count Loris-Melikov. To Virginsky's relief that secondment had come to an end and he had been moved to the Rozhdestvenskaya District, based mainly at the station on 2nd Rozhdestvenskaya Street. Not before time. The memory of his time at Fontanka Embankment stirred fierce and dangerous emotions. Loris-Melikov's machinations - and the murky dealings of the secret police - had resulted in two men's death. One of them was Ptitsyn, a good man and an excellent officer. In certain dreams, Virginsky could still see his eager and slightly earnest face turned mutely towards him. His expression was always one of implicit trust - a trust that Virginsky had betrayed. He would never be able to forgive himself for the part he had played in Ptitsyn's death.

For now, he consoled himself by taking his feelings out on Sergeant Petrov, who suffered from the insuperable disadvantage of not being Sergeant Ptitsyn. Virginsky had other reasons for disliking the man. His look was watchful and superior, as if he was waiting for Virginsky to slip up. Virginsky also suspected Petrov of habitually holding out on him for reasons that were not yet clear. Perhaps Virginsky's dealings with Loris-Melikov had made him distrustful.

Without doubt, there was something about Petrov that irritated Virginsky.

'You don't have the head,' Virginsky said flatly, though his words were loaded with weary disappointment.

Petrov guessed what Virginsky was driving at. 'His son-in-law identified him. There is a distinctive signet ring on the left hand.'

Virginsky crouched down to examine the ring. 'A rabbit.'

'Yes. It is General Krolikov's emblem.[1] As well as that, he says that the clothes and the cane, and the overall build of the body are consistent with his father-in-law. And he had gone missing, of course. The family were looking for him. They were celebrating his name day and he became separated from the group. His daughter had begun to grow concerned.'

Virginsky stood up and widened his eyes sceptically. 'He wandered off on his own on his name day? Shouldn't he have been

_____

1. Author's note: The name Krolikov is derived from krolik, the Russian for rabbit.

within the bosom of his loving family?'

'You can speak to them yourself and draw your own conclusions on that. I have merely noted the salient facts.'

Virginsky frowned, unsure how to interpret Petrov's tone. Was he perhaps kicking back against the magistrate's implied criticism. 'You must have formed some impressions?'

'My impression is that he was a cantankerous old man.'

'I see. Anyone within the family a likely suspect? This son-in-law, for instance?'

'Krolikov was wealthy. I expect there are many among them whom we may consider suspects. Though which of them stood to benefit from his death, we do not yet know.'

'You think it is to do with the inheritance?'

Petrov wrinkled his nose.

Despite his antagonism towards Petrov, Virginsky found himself in agreement. 'It's too extreme?'

'It's not the normal way that family members are bumped off. The inheritance murderer usually prefers poison.'

'To chop off the head... and then to take it. This is surely the work of a maniac?'

'Or someone who wants to make it look like a maniac.'

Virginsky snorted impatiently. 'Who found him, the son-in-law?'

'No. It was one -' Petrov consulted his notebook - 'Oznobishin. A trader in animal feed. A drunken trader, I should add. He keeps a warehouse in the Moskovskaya District. He has quite a tale to tell, if you wish to hear it.'

'All in good time.'

'The longer you leave it, the drunker he will get.'

'Can you not separate him from his means of intoxication?'

'This is Russia. The police here do not have the authority for that.'

Virginsky looked at Petrov sharply. Had he just made a joke? Virginsky was not in the mood for jokes. He stood up tall and took in the lie of the land.

'What happened here, sergeant?'

Petrov didn't answer, except to shake his head, once, tersely. He then took Virginsky through what he knew of General Krolikov's last moments. He pointed in the direction of the path where the general had last been seen by his daughter.

Virginsky stood over the body, his head angled as if he were listening for something, his gaze distant.

Not too far away, a musical performance was taking place. Families still promenaded along the paths of Tavrichesky Garden, or settled on the grass to picnic. The laughter and joyful cries of children playing reached him.

3

The medical examiner arrived, a taciturn German called Schloss. He nodded reticently to Virginsky, who moved away from the body to make way for him.

'Dr Schloss has been attending to the deceased's daughter,' Petrov said in a loud aside.

'Oh yes? How did you find her?'

The doctor shrugged. 'I gave her something to soothe her nerves.' That seemed to be all that Virginsky was going to get out of him.

Petrov filled in the details. 'I would say she is bearing up surprisingly well, considering. She has a daughter herself, a little girl, and so I believe she is determined to put a brave face on it for the sake of the child.'

'Has she seen her father… like this?'

'No. It was thought better to keep her away from the full horror of it. She has been informed of the circumstances, however. Do you wish to speak to her now? I have already taken a statement but I thought you would want to speak to her yourself. I believe it would be the kindest thing to release the family as soon as we are able.'

Virginsky declined to respond to Petrov's perfectly humane consideration. He took a moment longer to review the scene; his sole purpose was to impress on Petrov that he would not be rushed into any action. He alone would decide which witness to interview next and when.

Finally, he gave a terse nod and followed Petrov out of this chill, dark place of death and violence. They headed out towards a grassy bank, where a group of twenty or so people were clustered, their faces pale and bewildered in the lurid sunlight.

The older men and women shook their heads disconsolately. Younger ones talked in urgent whispers. One woman wailed in abject terror. The children sat open mouthed and dazed. Something momentous had happened in their young lives. Their parents were openly weeping, and that was bad enough, but they sensed something more than adult sorrow at work here: adult fear.

This was a day that would scar their souls forever.

Seated on the grass, a woman comforted a little girl of about six or seven, whose face was buried in her bosom. The woman's own face was streaked with tears. Next to her, a man hugged his knees and shook his head compulsively.

Petrov nodded. 'That's her. Vera Timofeevna Myasnikova. And that's her husband, Myasnikov.'

'The son-in-law.' Virginsky blew out his cheeks and strode over to the stricken family. 'Madam, my condolences for your loss. I am the investigating magistrate Virginsky. It is my duty to ask you some questions about… what happened here today. Perhaps…' Virginsky gave a sympathetic grimace and nodded towards her daughter.

The woman winced her eyes shut then gently tried to peel her daughter away from her. She bent her head and spoke in a low, soothing whisper. 'Come now, Danka. Go to Papa for a moment. Mama must speak to this gentleman.'

But Danka clung on, if anything tightening her grip on her mother's body. Her father stirred himself and tried to pull her away to him. The girl responded to his gentle pressure by howling as if he had struck her.

Myasnikov gave up his attempt and held up his hands helplessly.

Vera stroked her daughter's hair. 'You must be brave, Danka. You must be brave for Mama. You must be brave for Papa, too. Papa needs your love as much as I do.'

Eventually, the girl grew calmer and allowed herself to be handed over. Vera stood up and straightened her dress before walking a few paces away with Virginsky.

'Please be assured, we will do everything we can to catch the monster who did this to your father.'

Vera confronted him with steady, unblinking eyes, the pupils mere pinpoints. Virginsky wondered if this was the effect of whatever sedative Dr Schloss had given her.

'Is it true? His head is missing?'

'I'm afraid so.' Was it cruel to tell her this? It felt so. But it was the truth. Perhaps her husband had kept this detail from her, in

11

which case, who was Virginsky to break it to her?

Vera gave a sharp cry of anguish, which provoked her daughter to tear herself away from her father and coming running up to her. The little girl threw herself at her mother's legs.

'No, no, Danka. You must go back to Papa. It's all right. Mama is all right. Please. Papa needs you now.'

Myasnikov retrieved his daughter.

Vera squeezed her eyes tightly shut and held her breath, suppressing another cry. Finally, all that she would allow herself was a deep gasp, almost of wonder. She shook her head violently, as if to rid herself of her grief, then turned to face Virginsky again.

He stood with his head bowed, abashed before the woman's distress. He felt the need to say something, but could find no words.

'They would not let me see him.'

'I do not think it is advisable.'

'Who could have done this?'

'That is the very question we are determined to answer. With your help.'

'*My* help?'

'There is a question that it is customary to ask in circumstances like this.'

'What do you mean, circumstances like this? When are there ever circumstances like this?'

'I'm sorry. I did not express myself well. I mean, when one is investigating the crime of murder.'

Vera noisily snorted in the mucus that constantly threatened to escape from her nose.

'That question is, do you know of anyone who may have wanted your father dead? Did he have any enemies?'

'My father was much-loved.'

'You can think of no one?'

'No.'

'He was a military gentleman, I understand.'

'Retired.'

'Yes, of course. Perhaps there was someone from his past?'

'I know nothing of that part of my father's life. But I do know my father. He was a good man.'

'A good man may still have enemies. Especially if he was a warrior.'

'It was all a long time ago.'

'Today was his name day?'

'Yes. We came here with the whole family to celebrate with him.'

'Your father became separated from the rest of you, I believe.'

'Yes.'

'Why was that?'

'My father loved to forage for mushrooms. He was always wandering off without telling us.'

'Did you notice if anyone else was absent from the group?' On the face of it, the idea that the murderer was one of the name day party was unlikely. But he was obliged to explore every possibility. 'There is no one, for instance, who was gone for a long time, longer than anyone else? Or who is still missing now?'

Vera scowled at him threateningly. 'What are you suggesting? That one of his family did this to him?'

'I must look into everything. If only to eliminate suspects from my enquiry.'

She let out an aggrieved cry. 'Suspects!'

'I use the word technically, without any presumption of guilt.'

She shook out an angry denial. 'We were all together.'

'Until you noticed he was missing? Then, presumably, you split up to look for him. Separately.'

'I'm not sure. I don't remember. I suppose so.'

'If it were so, then there was a time when you were all out of each other's sight?'

'But no. It doesn't make sense! No one here has a weapon!' Her face lit up manically, electrified by the strange, dark energy that was coursing through her.

Hers was a reasonable objection. But not irrefutable. A weapon might have been concealed before the attack. And it may have been someone else who wielded it on behalf of a family member. A hired assassin, in other words. If that were the case, the peculiar methodology began to make sense.

Virginsky kept such thoughts to himself. 'Your father had made a will?'

'I believe so.'

'Who were the beneficiaries, do you know?'

'You think someone chopped off his head to get at his money?'

Virginsky did not answer.

Vera sighed impatiently. 'I… was… the main… beneficiary. So now, do you believe that I did it?'

Virginsky had the decency to shake his head.

But Vera was not to be so easily pacified. She held her arms out in front of her and screamed: 'Where is the blood? Would I not have blood on me?'

There was an agitated movement from the gathered family members. Virginsky felt their heads turn towards him with aggrieved hostility. Little Danka began to cry. Vera's husband came over, bristling with masculine aggression.

'What's going on?'

All at once, the energy went from Vera.

'Please accept my apologies. There are questions I am obliged to ask. I do not like to ask them but it is my duty to do so.'

'There is a madman on the loose and you are harassing my wife? She is grieving for her father!' Myasnikov shook his head in disgust.

Vera took advantage of his intervention to flee from Virginsky. He watched her scoop up her daughter and pull the child into her body with a desperate, cleaving love.

'We are doing what we can,' said Virginsky. 'I am merely trying to establish if there is anyone who may have had a reason to kill the general.'

'And you thought *she* did?'

'Not at all. Perhaps it would have been better to ask you the question. Did *you* know if he had any enemies.'

'I'm sure there were some. You don't get to that age without putting a few noses out of joint. But whether there is anyone who would do this…' Myasnikov pursed his lips decisively. 'Surely not. He is an old man. He would have been dead before long anyhow. What is the point?'

Virginsky handed over a card. 'If you think of anyone…'

'Can we go now?'

'Yes. Once again, please accept my condolences.'

As Myasnikov hurried off, Virginsky turned to Petrov who raised his eyebrows questioningly.

'What?' snapped Virginsky.

'I merely wondered if you're ready to talk to the man who found the body?'

Virginsky gave a terse, bad-tempered nod.

4

The merchant Oznobishin was slumped with his back against a tree, his eyes closed as if dozing. His face was turned upwards to take in what warmth he could from the wavering sun. He was a big man, broad as well as tall, wearing a loose blue and white striped overcoat, unbuttoned. The massy beard of a *muzhik* spilled out from the lower half of his face. In one hand, he clutched a bottle of vodka. He let the bottle rest against his thigh, as if he took comfort from its touch, as much as from its contents, which were almost spent.

He was humming tunelessly under his breath. A strong, unpleasant smell came from his sweating body.

'You, Oznobishin!' shouted Petrov.

Oznobishin opened his eyes and turned his head slowly.

'Stand up straight when you are in the presence of the magistrate.'

Oznobishin swayed unsteadily as he attempted to stand without the aid of the tree trunk. 'You will forgive me, your Excellency. I have received a terrible shock today. I am not usually to be found in this condition.'

Virginsky made a concessionary gesture with one hand. 'It's all right, Sergeant. He may lean against the tree if it is easier for him.'

'Your Excellency is too kind.' Oznobishin fell back and closed his eyes again.

'Open your eyes!' barked Petrov.

Oznobishin winced as the words struck him. He blinked and turned his torpid gaze towards Virginsky.

'You were the one who found the body?'

Oznobishin nodded wordlessly.

'Tell me what happened.'

'It is a tale of human frailty, your Excellency.'

'I am not an Excellency. If you wish to use an honorific, your Honour will suffice.'

'You are a democrat, I see. As are we all now, thanks to the reforms of the generous father Tsar.'

'Just tell the magistrate what happened!'

'Well, I am afraid to say, your Excellency, I shat myself.'

'Not that part.'

'Ah, yes, of course. Well, you see, your Excellency, I was taken short you see. It is a function that is common to all human beings, indeed, all animate creatures, and so there is no shame in it. However, I am not some uncouth peasant who does his business on the public byway. I am Osip Maximovich Oznobishin, a trader in animal feed.'

'Get on with it!' snapped Petrov.

'And so I ventured into the woods, seeking an appropriate place to evacuate that which was causing me discomfort.'

'You need not go into detail on that side of things,' said Virginsky.

'Just tell him what you saw!'

'I saw Sonya.'

'Sonya?'

'You know, Sonya in the Kingdom of Wonder.'

'It is a book for children, your Honour. My daughter has a copy of it. It is rather fantastical. It concerns the adventures of a little girl called Sonya in a strange land. It's quite eccentric. I believe it was written by an Englishman.'

Virginsky stared at Petrov, who seemed to lose his confidence.

Oznobishin nodded emphatically. 'That's right, Sonya. Only she wasn't dressed like Sonya. She was dressed like a Caucasian. Ornately so, I would say. Like a Caucasian bride, if you know what I mean. She was dressed in a gorgeous crimson gown, trimmed with gold. I don't remember Sonya being dressed like that in the story. But the book cannot tell us all the marvellous adventures she had.'

Virginsky's question was for Petrov. 'Do we think a little girl did this?'

'Tell him what else,' Petrov commanded.

'She was with the Mad Hatter.'

Virginsky's mystification must have shown in his face, as Petrov felt it necessary to explain: 'It is another character from the same book.'

'Sergeant, what is going on here?'

'Please, your Honour.' Petrov nodded encouragingly to Oznobishin.

'The Mad Hatter had a bag.'

'I see.'

'I said "Good day," and they did not answer. It seemed to me that they were in a hurry. And in the story, it is always the White Rabbit who is in a hurry. And then I came to the place where I found the White Rabbit, only his head was missing. That's when I shat myself.'

Virginsky said nothing.

'And then, after I had got my wits about me again, I thought, "Ah, I know who is behind this!"'

'You do?'

'Yes.'

'*Who*?'

'The Queen of Hearts. She must have ordered it. "Off with his head!" Isn't that what she always says? And the Mad Hatter has obliged. Which is why he was speckled with hearts.'

'Speckled with hearts?'

'He had red hearts on him. On his shirt front. It is the mark of the queen he serves.'

Petrov stirred excitedly. But Virginsky refused to find the information interesting.

Virginsky pointed back towards the spot where General Krolikov's body still lay. 'But it is not a rabbit,' he objected. 'It is a *man* who lies there.'

'The White Rabbit has a man's body and a rabbit's head,' said Petrov. 'What I mean to say is, not that the victim is the White Rabbit. Obviously not. I am merely trying to explain this man's logic.'

'You use the word logic in a way that I do not understand.'

'Your Honour, leaving aside the more outlandish elements of his account, do you not believe it possible that he saw something, even though he does not understand what he saw? Perhaps there really was a man in a top hat, carrying a bag, accompanied by a little girl, dressed in a Caucasian costume. The red hearts, well… I think you know what that could be. Perhaps it was Krolikov's head in the bag?'

'Yes!' cried Oznobishin excitedly. 'It was his head! It was the White Rabbit's head! In the bag!'

'Do you think, Sergeant Petrov, in the unlikely event that this witness's testimony should lead us to our murderer, that I will be able to make use of it in a court of law? Can you picture *him* on the stand?'

Petrov looked crestfallen.

'You,' Virginsky addressed the drunken trader sharply. 'Where did this encounter take place?'

'It was in the trees. Over there.' Oznobishin gestured vaguely.

'And did you see which way they went, this Sonya and… the other one?'

Oznobishin stuck out his right arm with such force that he almost fell over. 'That way.'

'No, no, no!' cried Petrov. 'That's not what you told me earlier. You said they were heading west, which is that way.' Petrov pointed in the opposite direction to Oznobishin.

Virginsky's mouth curled into an unworthy smirk at Petrov's embarrassment.

'Yes, that's right,' agreed Oznobishin. 'That way. That's what I said, that way.' And now he pointed with equal certainty in a third direction.

Virginsky turned to Petrov. 'You have looked for these individuals?'

'Without success, your Honour.'

Virginsky scowled in dissatisfaction at Oznobishin. 'Did any *other* witnesses see them?'

'There have been no other sightings so far.'

'So they just disappeared?'

'Yes! Yes!' cried Oznobishin. 'Down a rabbit hole!'

Virginsky shook his head despairingly. 'Is this all we have?'

'At the moment, yes, your Honour.'

'Then we have nothing.'

Virginsky turned sharply and walked away.

5

Virginsky took the lie of the land, pacing the terrain where the victim had been found. In truth, he wasn't entirely sure what he was looking for. To make it worse, he sensed his every step watched over and scrutinised. The grey eminences had begun to gather, drawn by the horrific nature of the crime. Virginsky recognised the Chief Superintendent of the Rozhdestvenskaya Police District, Volkov, who did his best to live up to his name by sniffing the air like a wolf, as if he believed he could pick up the murderer's scent. Virginsky expected him to throw back his head and howl at any moment. Next to Volkov was the City Governor, Gresser, who wrung his hands and shook his head despondently. He had the look of a man who did not expect to be in the job for long. *First the bomb blast at the Winter Palace, now this!* was no doubt going through his mind. The *prokuror*, Liputin, cast stern, disobliging glances in Virginsky's direction, as if he knew very well who was to blame.

Liputin stood a little shorter than he once had, stooped and shrunk by age, though he was still as immaculately turned out as ever, and just as intimidating. He was clearly a man who placed great emphasis on appearances; Virginsky would even go so far as to say the *prokuror* saw the function of the justice system as maintaining them. In the past, this had brought him into conflict with Virginsky's old mentor, Porfiry Petrovich, who distrusted appearances and liked to get behind them, even if it meant exposing an inconvenient truth. The *prokuror* had transferred his dislike of the great investigator onto Virginsky.

But official interest went even higher than those three distinguished individuals. Also in attendance was Nabokov, the Justice Minister, and Makov, Minister of the Interior. They eyed each other with a complex mixture of wariness and disdain, as if they each knew something damaging about the other but were afraid of what the other knew about them.

Of course, the sensational and terrifying nature of the crime explained the interest of these higher-ups. St Petersburg was jumpy enough as it was already. Once the news of the attack got out, it would send shockwaves through society. Could it justifiably be considered an act of terror? The status of the victim, the time and location of his murder - in a public park, on his name day, surrounded by his family, with other members of the public close by - all of that would contribute to a general sense of fear, if not horror.

The psychological impact of the attack could not be underestimated. If it could happen to General Krolikov, it could happen to anyone.

There was also the possibility of a political aspect to the crime, as Virginsky was obliged to acknowledge. Was Krolikov aligned with one of the factions that were grappling for influence behind the scenes? Was he an important enough individual to warrant a political assassination? If so, Virginsky was not aware of it.

Even if it was not a political crime, the result might still be civil unrest. The general supineness of the populace, which the government relied on to be able to get on with its business, would be disturbed.

No wonder these men looked worried.

Certainly, it did not have the hallmark of the People's Will, whose terrorists generally preferred dynamite and pistols, as the tools by which they carried out their revolution. A sword - if sword it was that had been wielded against the general - was altogether too aristocratic a weapon. It suggested cavalry officer rather than revolutionary. Perhaps the fatal blow had been delivered by a former comrade of Krolikov's? An act of revenge, which had at its roots some question of honour. It was always honour, or the loss of it, with these military types.

At any rate, it seemed that news of General Krolikov's murder had gone all the way to the top - well almost. At least now that Count Loris-Melikov had starved the Third Section of oxygen, there were no gendarmes involved. The department was a spent force, after Loris-Melikov had exposed how it had been working in league with the Tsar's domestic enemies, almost as a state within a state. Virginsky had played a part in that. And two men were dead now because of it.

Once again, Virginsky found himself brooding on the man who had manipulated him into a dangerous situation, from which he had been lucky to escape with his life.

He contrasted his own view of Loris-Melikov with the public perception.

Loris-Melikov had wooed the newspaper editors, who were already calling him the Dictator of the Heart. Virginsky knew better. To him, Loris-Melikov was a cold-blooded puppet master. It was all a game to him. He was as capable of sacrificing human lives as he was pawns on a chessboard.

He was presented as a benign administrator who would restore the capital - and the Empire - to peace and good order by taking away the grievances of the disaffected. It was a clever strategy. Give the agitators what they want - democracy, in other words - and they will stop agitating. At the very least, you turn the public against them.

And so, Loris-Melikov was leading the Tsar towards a constitution. The only problem was there were those on the right, the Tsar's own son for one, who were determined to stop this lurch away from absolute power. And they would do anything, including working in league with terrorists, to preserve the autocracy in its purest form.

Loris-Melikov was equally determined, and equally ruthless, on the side of progress.

This placed Virginsky in a bind. He supported Loris-Melikov's aims, but had seen first-hand the damage caused by his unscrupulous methods.

Virginsky wondered bitterly how soon it would be before the head of the Administrative Council himself would condescend to take an interest in this present case.

In the event, he did not have long to wait.

The important personages formed a curved barrier that seemed to be closing in slowly on Virginsky. All at once, the barrier broke, and the personages scattered, like pigeons in the presence of an eagle. That eagle was Count Loris-Melikov.

'My dear Pavel Pavlovich, how good to see you again, even it is under these less than propitious circumstances.'

Loris-Melikov's eyes bulged with that peculiar alert intensity that Virginsky had noticed in their earlier meetings. The count's side whiskers and moustaches were every bit as luxuriant as he remembered them, perhaps even more wild and unruly.

'Your Excellency.'

'It is a terrible business, is it not?'

Virginsky bowed his head in acknowledgement.

'We are fortunate to be able to call on an investigator of your talents at a time like this. The Tsar has asked me to convey to you his gratitude for your help in that other matter. He is grateful - as are we all - that this investigation has fallen to you.'

Virginsky knew that the Tsar's gratitude was never a simple matter. And it was, after all, gratitude given in anticipation. He had not done anything to earn it yet.

'Did the Tsar know General Krolikov?'

'Who did not know General Krolikov?'

Virginsky frowned in confusion. 'I confess, I did not, before today.'

'I meant, who of consequence. You will not be offended.' It was a strange order.

'So, he was an important man?'

'Pavel Pavlovich, will you walk with me?' Loris-Melikov placed one arm around Virginsky's shoulder. Virginsky felt himself shrink from the man's dubious protection. But the Dictator of the Heart was insistent. He led Virginsky away from the resentful curiosity of the slightly less important personages.

As soon as they were out of earshot, Loris-Melikov began: 'There is one aspect of this case that you do not understand.'

Virginsky widened his eyes, until he felt that they must be bulging almost as much as Loris-Melikov's. There were many responses he could have given to Loris-Melikov's assertion. For example, he could have blurted, 'Only *one* thing?' But he did not. He held his peace and nodded for the count to go on.

'General Krolikov was a member of the Anichkov Palace grouping.'

'I knew it!'

Loris-Melikov's eyes stood out even more, if that were possible.

'You did?'

'That is to say, I suspected there might be some political angle to this. I didn't know what his alignment was, but I knew he must have been aligned to something.'

'And how did you work that out?'

Virginsky was reluctant to take Loris-Melikov into his confidence. That had not ended well the last time he had done so. But he could hardly refuse to answer the dictator's question. He reminded himself that he was an investigating magistrate, and that he had a job to do. 'What is the most striking aspect of this murder?'

'The decapitation?'

'Yes. And not only that. It was not enough to cut the head off. It had to be taken away.'

'What do you conclude from that?'

'Two possibilities. The first, we are dealing with a hired assassin. The head was taken away as proof of contract fulfilment.'

'But surely there would be no need for that? The general's murder will be all over the next editions of the papers.'

'Possibly. Generally speaking, professional assassins have their habitual working methods, which they tend to stick to, no matter what.'

Loris-Melikov pursed his lips thoughtfully. 'What is the second possibility?'

'There is a maniac on the loose. In which case, the head was taken away as a trophy.'

'I incline towards your first hypothesis, although I do not think the removal of the head was for the reason you suggest.'

'Oh?'

'Of course, I am not a detective…'

'No.' It was strange. Despite all the reasons Virginsky had for hating Loris-Melikov, he found himself drawn into his orbit, once again. 'Even so, I would be interested to hear your theory. Excellency.'

'This was done to send a message.'

Virginsky dipped his head for the other man to continue.

'Let us try to get inside the minds of the Anichkov Palace

Faction. Following the suicide of one of its leading lights… Major Verkhotsev, you remember?'

Virginsky nodded tersely. In truth, how could he forget. He had been there when it happened. And he had been the one to break the news to Verkhotsev's daughter, Maria Petrovna, a young woman in whose well-being he held a deep interest.

'It is reasonable to suspect that they are in disarray. We may even go so far as to say, in turmoil. They begin to mistrust one another. To turn on one another. Krolikov was an old man. He was becoming unreliable. Indiscreet. He said things without realising he was speaking.' Loris-Melikov tapped his temple. 'Senile, I'm afraid.'

'You think one of the Tsarevich's loyalists did this? To silence him?'

'They may not have inflicted the fatal blow themselves. As you suggest, a hired assassin may be involved. And the motive was not exactly to silence him. Or not only. Rather to warn others. A message, as I say.'

'Don't lose your heads.'

'You could put it like that. I prefer to say, close ranks and keep the faith.'

'It seems an excessive way to ensure loyalty.'

'Make no mistake, for these people, this is a matter of life and death. And the death they want more than any other is the Tsar's.'

Virginsky said nothing. He had the sense that Loris-Melikov was about to get to the point.

'Here's what I want you to do, my friend. I want you to infiltrate the Anichkov Palace faction and find out what's going on there.'

'How will I do that?'

'You'll find a way, I'm sure.'

'But won't they know that I am associated with you?'

'I knew I could count on you!'

'I'm sorry, I don't…?'

'That is your way in. You go to them offering to spy on me!'

'I am not sure they will believe that.'

'You have to make them believe it, Pavel Pavlovich. You must express your dissatisfaction with the work of the Special

Commission. If necessary, give vent to feelings of the utmost detestation towards me personally. You have my permission to malign me in whatever manner occurs to you. You may call me a… a… an unscrupulous devil, or such like.'

'I think it will have to be stronger than that, your Excellency.'

'I'll leave it to you. Also, you must give them something, of course. I will provide you with some compromising material which you can say you have stolen from me.'

'And then what?'

'And then you report back to me on exactly what it is they're plotting.'

Virginsky narrowed his eyes. 'Won't that be dangerous? I mean, if you're right about who's behind General Krolikov's murder?'

'The Tsar's gratitude will be immeasurable.'

Virginsky thought he detected a faint, complacent smile on Loris-Melikov's face.

'You will do it?'

'First, I have a case to investigate.'

'Ah, my friend, I'm confident you will solve that mystery before too long. There'll be a breakthrough soon, I'm sure of it.'

'Your confidence flatters me.'

Loris-Melikov folded his body into a deep bow. Virginsky flinched from the gesture, as if from some regrettable lapse in taste.

6

Virginsky watched the uniformed officers fan out as they scoured the ground. They were looking for a weapon, though Virginsky had little expectation that they would find anything. If this was a professional assassination, it was unlikely that the killer would leave behind one of the valuable tools of his trade, especially as it was also a vital piece of evidence that could lead the police to him.

If his other theory was correct, and this was the work of a madman... well, in that case, it all depended on what kind of madman you were dealing with. The mad are famously unpredictable, so it was always possible that the killer might have discarded the weapon in the frenzy and elation of the attack. But somehow that did not chime with Virginsky's instincts.

This did not seem to be a disorganised killing. Either Krolikov was deliberately targeted or he was chosen at random. Either way, the murderer had lain in wait for his victim. He had come to the gardens today with the intention of killing.

The fact that the killer had taken the head away suggested a retentive nature. He had retrieved a token. By doing so, he was keeping the full atrocity of the crime to himself. Virginsky had the sense of someone jealously guarding the most significant items associated with the horrific deed, which he would see as his finest accomplishment. Just as he would have taken pleasure from possessing the severed head, he would have been unwilling to relinquish the means by which he had attained it.

Although he had been dismissive of Oznobishin's evidence, he couldn't get the image of a top hatted figure and a Caucasian child out of his head. However drunk the trader was, it seemed unlikely that he would make up such an odd couple. He must have seen something. And the detail of the red hearts on the Mad Hatter's shirt was intriguing. It sounded very much like the man's addled intellect had tried to make sense of blood spatter.

It seemed to be the case that the head had been detached with a single strike, though he would have to await the medical examiner's report for confirmation of that. The blow would have

27

to have been delivered with great skill. It would have required a powerful weapon, a massive, well-balanced sword, for example, or a long-handled executioner's axe. It would have to be something that could be swung with tremendous force, in order to attain the necessary momentum.

But Oznobishin had said nothing about seeing such a weapon on either of these two mysterious individuals. Virginsky tried to picture the scene that Oznobishin had described. The trader had mentioned something about a bag but he had not remarked on it being particularly long. It seemed unlikely that the murder weapon could have been contained in that, especially if there was also a head in there.

If this Mad Hatter was the killer, then Virginsky was forced to revise his theories, or at least expand the number of possibilities he was prepared to consider. He conceded that it was possible that the killer had stolen into the park at night in order to hide the weapon in advance, so that he would not be seen carrying something that would surely draw unwanted attention. In which case, perhaps he had also hidden it somewhere after the deed was done?

The image of a hollow tree with a sword concealed inside it came to him.

Virginsky went back to the killing ground and stood in the centre of the small dark clearing, before turning 360 degrees.

The ground was rough and overgrown. In some places the grass appeared to be trodden down, but the impressions did not form themselves into any clear footprints from which casts could be taken. Nor did they seem to lead in any particular direction. And the more Virginsky looked at them, the less sure he was that they were evidence of human tread - or of anything at all. They seemed to spring up and disappear, to be replaced by other undulations elsewhere that could equally be caused by someone walking there. Or not. If he turned away from one of them, he had trouble finding it again afterwards.

Oznobishin could not be relied on for the location of his encounter with the Mad Hatter and Sonya, if it happened at all. In truth, he could not be relied on for anything. But assuming for a moment that he had met someone, and that someone was General Krolikov's murderer, it was unlikely that they would be heading back to the main path.

Virginsky stood with his back towards the path and walked straight ahead of him. When he reached the tree line, he noticed that one of the branches from an oak tree had been cleanly severed at about chest height. He looked down and found the end of the branch on the ground.

The cut looked fresh. The inner flesh of the tree was bright and unweathered. He looked about for blood spots but found none. He imagined the murderer exhilarated by his recent crime, fearless, invulnerable, brooking no obstacle to his fierce will. One swift flourish of his deadly blade before sheathing it (or whatever it was that he did with it) and the feeble branch was gone.

He pressed on. The interlocking branches resisted his progress, but finally yielded, before closing the way behind him. There was no path as such, but someone had pushed through here before him, and recently. He felt certain of it.

Virginsky kept his gaze angled down towards the bases of the trees. He tried to ignore the feeling that he was engaged in a hopeless quest, looking for the wind in the field, in the words of the proverb. But none of the uniformed police had come this way, presumably because they thought it was impassable, and so at least he was not doubling up on their efforts.

He had not shared his idea with anyone. If he found nothing, at least he wouldn't lose face.

Just as he was thinking this, he came to the very thing he had pictured: the trunk of an old, dead tree in which a narrow, ogive-ended gap opened on a hollow interior.

Virginsky dropped onto his haunches and peered inside.

7

At first sight, the tree appeared empty. There was certainly no sign of a weapon in there, no metallic glint cutting through the gloom of the dank interior. A large spider scuttled frantically over the rim of the opening, disappearing inside. Virginsky noticed the strands of a web, intact at the bottom, but broken above. Could that be evidence of someone reaching in? If so, they must have done so recently, otherwise the spider would have rebuilt her web.

He gingerly offered his own hand into the mouth of the gap. If there was an exposed blade out of sight, he did not want to cut himself on it. His extended fingers met no resistance, and so he lowered his hand slowly, destroying what was left of the web. The hollow interior continued below the lower edge of the opening.

At last his reach met resistance, a soft and slightly damp something. He pulled out a large towel, heavily bloodstained.

Virginsky stood. 'Petrov!'

A moment later he heard the sound of scrambling coming from the direction of the clearing. 'Over here!' The scrambling grew more frantic. 'Be careful there! This is a crime scene, remember. It's important to preserve it as much as we are able.'

Petrov burst through the branches with a furious oath. Virginsky met his discomfiture with an ironically solicitous expression. The other man's scowl was almost threatening.

Virginsky held up the bloody cloth.

Petrov's face lit up with surprise. 'Well, well, well. Where did you find that?'

'Inside this tree.'

Petrov nodded, impressed, his earlier annoyance forgotten. There was nothing like a piece of bloody evidence to restore one's spirits.

'The blood is still damp.'

But now Petrov sucked his teeth discouragingly. It was almost as if he considered it his duty to cast doubt on whatever advances Virginsky made. 'There is no way of knowing if it is General Krolikov's blood. Or even human. Dr Schloss may be able to narrow it down to mammals.'

Virginsky held the towel open, revealing a number of rough, elongated smears, as well as more formless stains. One mark looked superficially like a handprint. 'It is Krolikov's blood. I believe the killer used it to wipe clean the blade of the fatal weapon. He may also have wiped blood from his face. Remember, Oznobishin said that the Mad Hatter had red hearts on his shirt front, but he mentioned nothing about his face.'

'Ah, so now you are inclined to believe in my Mad Hatter!'

'He is not your Mad Hatter. And as you know, one must proceed only where the evidence leads. Uncorroborated, Oznobishin's statement could barely even be considered evidence.' Virginsky looked down at the towel. 'Hold out your hand.'

'You do not think I -?'

'Please, just put it next to this mark. I want to check something.'

'Well?'

'Do you have particularly large hands?'

'They are respectably proportioned, I would say.'

'But average? For a man?'

'I suppose so. What of it?'

Virginsky shook his head dubiously. 'There's probably nothing in it.' Under his breath, he added: 'I wonder if Dr Schloss will be able to make anything of this.'

Petrov narrowed his eyes and bent over to examine the stain more closely. 'I see what you mean. It's quite small. Almost like a child's.'

The two men looked at each other for a moment.

'Sonya,' said Petrov at last.

Virginsky pursed his lips sceptically. 'I am not even sure it is a handprint. As you say, it is too small.'

'It's Sonya,' insisted Petrov.

Virginsky was equally adamant. 'A child did not do this.'

'But a child may have got blood on her hands.'

'And the murderer wiped them clean?' Virginsky shook his head. 'What kind of assassin takes a child with them on a killing?'

Petrov offered no answer. He crouched down to examine the tangle of branches and twigs surrounding them from a lower

31

perspective. He appeared engrossed in peering into the twigs, but evidently his mind was elsewhere. 'So, what did he want, old Wolf's-Jaw-Fox's-Tail?' This was the name that some journalists had given Count Loris-Melikov, due to his well-known strategy of winning enemies over either by clever conciliation or, failing that, ruthless oppression.

'He's taking an interest in the case.'

'Any particular reason?'

Virginsky made a non-committal gesture. What he hated most about Loris-Melikov's intrigues was the way they drew you in. He was now obliged to lie, or at least be less than frank, with the officers working under him. 'Why do you think?' Virginsky was inclined to leave his answer there but was afraid that it wouldn't satisfy Petrov. 'This is an exceptionally brutal crime, perpetrated against a notable member of the establishment, an ex-soldier with a distinguished military record. We may consider it an act of terror. It's disruptive, destabilising. The powers-that-be are bound to want it resolved as soon as possible.'

'There is nothing more specific to his interest?'

Virginsky shook his head dismissively. 'Have your men focus on this area for now. Let me know if you find anything.'

'Where are you going?'

'I have something to attend to.'

'Something to do with Loris-Melikov?'

Virginsky was beginning to find Petrov's questioning impertinent. 'You have your instructions. There is no need of my presence here.'

With that, he pushed his way through the intertwined branches back towards the path.

8

Maria Petrovna Verkhotseva's small, unofficial school for working children was located in Rozhdestvenskaya District, a few streets south of Tavrichesky Garden. Since his transfer, Virginsky had not visited the school once. He could say that he had had no reason to go there. But he knew that he was avoiding her.

As Virginsky pushed open the street door, he heard children's voices raised in song. It was the sound he would always associate with the school. And with Maria Petrovna herself.

He smiled as he climbed the stairs to her classroom, though the image of General Krolikov's decapitated body repeatedly forced itself on him. He had a sense of two worlds existing side by side, one of evil and violence, the other of goodness and hope. Was he seeking refuge in Maria Petrovna's clean, wholesome presence from the appalling horror he had confronted? If only it were that simple.

Most classes were held in the afternoon, to enable the children to work their shifts at the factories. Virginsky had timed his visit to coincide with the end of the school day, hoping to catch her before she left for the evening.

The song came to an end as he reached the door of her classroom. He heard her firm voice address the children, calling them to order. It was miraculous, to him, how easily she controlled them. She was stricter than he expected, but the children accepted it from her. They hung on her every word.

There was a clatter of slates, then the clang of a handbell signalled the end of the lesson and the day.

Virginsky stood to one side as the children filed noisily out, their faces grimed with the soot from their working lives. Not all of them had shoes, and their clothes were frayed and dirty. Virginsky pitied them. But Maria Petrovna did something far more useful. She educated them.

Maria Petrovna was seated at her desk, her head bowed over an open book. She had not heard him come in.

The last time he had seen Maria, it was to tell her about her father's suicide. He had come away from that encounter burdened with guilt at his part in Verkhotsev's death. Not that she had said anything to accuse him, nor was there the slightest flicker of rebuke in her look.

Clearly, she had been overwhelmed by shock. Her soul was drowned in a sudden cascade of grief, her mind thrown into turmoil. Her complicated relationship with her father only added to her confusion.

He remembered her cry: 'How can I tell Mother this?' Even in the midst of her own suffering, it was someone else's feelings that she was thinking of.

Virginsky had stayed away from the funeral. He would like to say out of discretion, but really it was cowardice. He had imagined Maria turning on him with a righteous fury. 'You forced him to this!' she might justifiably have cried.

And he would have had no defence.

He cleared his throat. She lifted her head inquisitively, the frown of concentration still in place. There was a moment in which her expression froze, stricken by the same grief he had seen there once before. He realised that to her, he would always be associated with the moment she learnt of her father's death. Perhaps that was all he would ever be to her, the bearer of bad news.

But then her expression softened, and to his joy, he found that she had a smile for him. 'My dear Pavel Pavlovich!'

He cherished that 'dear'. But almost simultaneously was aware that he did not deserve it.

She must have seen something shadow his expression, as her own grew sombre to mirror it. 'What is it?' Unspoken was the charge: *What have you come to tell me this time?*

He mumbled an apology and ventured a smile of his own. 'No, nothing, I... merely wished... to see you... to see how you were...'

'You have been a stranger to me.' The rebuke was there, but it was gentle.

Virginsky blushed and avoided her gaze. And then he lifted his head and dared to look into her pale blue eyes, his heart devoid of hope.

'Maria Petrovna.' As he said her name, the welling emotions that had threatened him earlier burst their banks and flooded through him. He broke down, sobbing.

Maria leapt up from behind her desk and rushed towards him. She enveloped him in her arms. He welcomed her unquestioning warmth, as if he was already redeemed. But again, he knew that her compassion was unearned.

He began to gently pull away from her embrace, though he had not yet had enough of the comfort of her touch.

'There is something I have to tell you. It concerns your father.'

She closed her eyes on him, as if blocking out the sight of something offensive.

'At the time of his death, he was under investigation. He was suspected of feeding information to the terrorists. A trap was laid to catch him. That's why he took his own life.'

Her eyes were open again, her gaze stark and uncompromising. 'Why are you telling me this?'

'I was involved in that investigation.'

'Involved?'

Virginsky hid his face in his hands. 'I was there when he…'

'I see.'

He dropped his hands and faced her with as much candour as he could muster. 'I swear to you, Maria. I had no idea that it would end like that.'

'Were you the one?'

Virginsky frowned questioningly.

'The one who set the trap?'

He shook his head. 'No, I only learnt about the details of that when it was too late.' But Virginsky was determined not to let himself off the hook so easily. 'I should have known. I should never have got involved. I should have stopped it.' But there was something bogus about those statements. He had never had any agency in the business, had never had any choice in his actions, or control over the outcome. Perhaps that was what upset him most. His regret was over his powerlessness. 'I should have warned your father.' By now, the conviction had gone from his voice entirely.

'It is a hard thing for a child to bear when a parent takes their own life. Why has he done this? How could he do it to me? Yes, to *me*! How selfish I was in my grief. All I could think about was my pain and how cruel my father was to abandon me. It felt like a betrayal. He had a duty - did he not? - to keep faith, for my sake, if he could not do it for himself. And what of my mother? You did not come to the funeral. You did not see her tears or hear her weeping. I don't blame you. It was a hard thing to bear. It is one thing for a wife to find out that her husband has been unfaithful. But this betrayal is the worst betrayal of all. It's not just that he would rather be with another woman. He would rather be dead than be with her. It is a cruel blow. It is the cruelty of suicide that is hardest to bear.'

'He was driven to it. He believed he had no choice. He did not do it to hurt you or your mother.'

'Still, we were hurt. We were destroyed. He came to see me, you know. Here. Just before he did it. He told me that he was proud of me. Of what I had achieved here. He told me that it redeemed him. That it redeemed everyone!'

'It does.'

She gave an almost indignant laugh. 'No! You must find your own redemption. I am not Christ!'

'I don't want you to be!'

'Why have you come here, Pavel Pavlovich?'

'To ask your forgiveness.'

'You didn't kill him. He killed himself. You're not responsible.'

Virginsky pushed a hand through his hair. Her voice sounded harsh, belying the absolution implicit in her words.

'Unless there is something you are not telling me?'

Had she detected something secretive in his expression? His gaze flitted guiltily.

'You want something from me. That's why you're here.'

'Your father was a member of the Anichkov Palace faction.'

'What of it?'

'They, I believe, forced him to his death. Made it impossible for him to continue. They gave him no choice.'

'And so?'

'If I may be allowed to examine his private papers, perhaps I can find out who was responsible.'

'Is that why you came here today? This is all part of some investigation?'

'I only wish to find out the truth. About your father's death.'

'Why do I not believe you? Why do I think there is more to it than that?'

'Another man has died, who is also connected to the Anichkov Palace faction.'

Maria Petrovna shook her head slowly, sadly. 'What a fool I am!'

'No one who knows you would ever call you a fool.'

'I thought you had come to see me. But no, it was simply to get to my father's papers!'

Virginsky was shamed into silence.

'Please go.' Maria Petrovna turned and walked slowly to her desk, where she continued to stand with her back to Virginsky.

As he left the classroom, Virginsky let out a despondent sigh. What a shabby and deceitful individual he was! He had come here to manipulate her, like a poor man's Loris-Melikov! The thought disgusted him.

Well, at least he knew himself a little better now.

9

The next day, Virginsky was at his desk early. He found Dr Schloss's preliminary report waiting for him. It was written in Schloss's usual laconic style. That was as it should be. What was the point of literary flourishes in a medical examiner's report? The only thing that Virginsky objected to was Schloss's habit of giving his measurements in metric units rather than the Russian system of *arshin, fut* and *dyuym*. Virginsky had complained about this practice numerous times, and so now Schloss usually included a converted Russian measurement in parenthesis. This time he had forgotten to do so, presumably because he had written his report in a hurry.

It was frustrating because the report included an interesting discussion that depended on a precise understanding of the measurements involved.

Unsurprisingly, the doctor gave the cause of death as decapitation. The head had been removed by a single blow from a bladed weapon, in Schloss's opinion a military sword. The wound was clean and precise, suggesting the blade was extremely sharp and the individual wielding it highly skilled. The fatal blow ran from left to right, from the victim's point of view, which led Schloss to conclude that the attacker was probably right-handed. The surface of the severed neck lay at an angle, being lower at the front than the back by approximately 30 degrees.

This was where the interesting discussion began, because, according to Dr Schloss, it was possible from this angle to calculate the height of the assassin. There was a digression on the dimensions of human heads. As the general's was missing, it was impossible to state with certainty what his full height was. But the important measurements were the height of the body without the head - the height to the surface of the neck stump, in other words - and the angle that the blade had formed in making its cut.

Schloss prefaced his calculations by stating the assumptions he had based them on. If any of these assumptions were wrong, then his conclusions were meaningless. His most important assumption was that the assailant had been standing straight up, with his arms held straight, locked at the elbows. This would enable him to put the maximum force into wielding the sword, which would be necessary to ensure that the head was removed with a single blow.

Krolikov was a man of above average height. If he had been struck by someone significantly taller than him, the angle of the wound would have been higher at the front than the back. If his killer was roughly the same height, the wound would have been more or less level (though because the arms come from the shoulders, which are lower than the neck, it would in fact have been angled slightly downwards). But the angle of this wound was notably sharper than the horizontal, suggesting that the assassin was considerably shorter than Krolikov.

It was a matter of geometry. Schloss drew a simple figure to scale, with a vertical line representing General Krolikov's height (without his head). He then drew a line downwards from that at an angle of 30 degrees. The length of the assailant's arms and the length of the sword were unknown, but they could be estimated within certain ranges. The arm length was a variable correlating to the subject's height, as yet an unknown. Also unknown was the point along the sword's blade at which the neck had been struck, which was a more significant measurement than the overall length of the sword.

Essentially, you could mark a point anywhere along that downward line which would give you a possible shoulder height for the killer. The further along the line you placed the point, the shorter the assailant was. There was a reasonable minimum and maximum range for the position of this point, based on Schloss's knowledge of the average length of arms and a reasonable assumption about sword blades. From that point, you could draw a second vertical line, by measuring which and scaling it up, and then adding an estimated measurement for the head, you could arrive at a possible height for the murderer.

Schloss gave a range of projected heights, which as they were in centimetres were not immediately meaningful to Virginsky.

As for the towel, as expected, Dr Schloss was not able to confirm that the blood staining it came from the victim. He could only say that it was mammalian. He would not commit to identifying the mark that Virginsky had found as a hand print. It could equally have been caused by the manner in which the towel had been balled up.

Virginsky called in his clerk, Zamyotov, who at Virginsky's request had transferred with him from Stolyarny Lane. With his arch manner and barely-veiled sarcasm, Zamyotov had always been a slight irritant to Virginsky. But he had to acknowledge that the man was good at his job, and after the turmoil of his time at the Third Section, he had felt the need for continuity with his former life. And for all Zamyotov's foibles, he had proven himself someone Virginsky could trust. In uncertain times, when he could barely trust the ground he walked on, that was something he valued.

The clerk poked his head around the door with a quizzical, faintly ironic expression.

'Alexander Grigorevich, will you send a telegram to Dr Schloss at the Prince of Oldenburg's Hospital, requesting him to supply the measurements in his report in Russian units, please?' The Prince of Oldenburg's was a children's hospital, but it was the largest hospital in the Rozhdestvenskaya District. Schloss was known to be a competent pathologist, except for this peculiar foible.

'Oh, dear. He still insists on converting us all to metric, does he?'

'I'm afraid so.'

'You know there is a calculation you can do?'

'I don't have time for that.'

'No of course not. You would far rather send me running to the telegram office.'

Virginsky did not respond to Zamyotov's goading, dismissing his clerk with a distracted frown as he returned to studying Schloss's report.

A moment later, there was a knock at his door and Sergeant Petrov came in.

'Well, here's something.'

'What?'

'That fellow, Oznobishin.'

'What about him?'

'He's turned himself over and confessed.'

'Confessed to what?'

'To murdering General Krolikov, of course. What else?'

'Not possible.'

'It is. We're holding him downstairs. Do you want to speak to him?'

Virginsky sighed deeply. He held Petrov with a sceptical glare, before shaking his head in dissatisfaction. And yet, he could hardly refuse, despite the sinking feeling that Oznobishin was about to take him even further into the Kingdom of Wonder.

10

Oznobishin was seated at Petrov's desk, surrounded by the hustle and bustle of a busy police station. There was no one watching him and he was not handcuffed. It would have been an easy matter for him to slip away in Petrov's absence. But he was evidently not interested in making his escape.

A whiff of liquor hung about him, but the foul smell that had emanated from him yesterday was gone. He must have changed his trousers, though Virginsky noticed he was still wearing the same light-coloured striped overcoat. His face was pale, puffy and moist, and reminded Virginsky of a plate of rinsed tripe. His eyes had shrunk to pinpricks. Looking at him, you had the feeling that he'd had a bad night, that he had probably slept in his clothes, if at all, and that now he was suffering from a splitting headache. How he had managed to present himself at the station so early was a miracle.

And yet a peculiar energy infected him, as if he were reacting to the bites of tiny creatures in the seams of his clothes, which he may well have been. He was supposedly a tradesman, but things had clearly not been going well for him. Virginsky asked himself, *why had the man been wasting his time at Tavrichesky Garden, when presumably he had a business to run?*

Virginsky pulled up a chair and sat down facing Oznobishin. He waited for a while without speaking. Eventually, Oznobishin stilled his fidgeting and gave the magistrate his attention.

'What's this nonsense?' demanded Virginsky.

Oznobishin was clearly indignant at the line Virginsky's questioning had taken. 'It's not nonsense.'

'It's nonsense!' insisted Virginsky, allowing some of Petrov's sharpness to enter his voice.

Oznobishin jumped a little in his seat.

'So, it was you who killed General Krolikov?'

'Yes.'

'Why did you not bring this up yesterday when we spoke to you?'

'I was afraid.'

'And now you are not afraid?'

'No, I am still afraid. But it has been a burden on my soul.'

'What is General Krolikov to you?'

'He is one of them.'

'One of whom?'

Oznobishin stabbed his own temple sharply with the tips of two fingers.

Virginsky shrugged, non-plussed. 'What is that supposed to mean? That he was mad?'

'Inside his head. It was different. He didn't have a brain. I mean, a human brain.'

'What in God's name are you talking about?'

'It was like a clock.'

'A clock?'

'Yes.'

'You mean a clockwork mechanism?'

'Yes. He had to wind it up, otherwise…' Oznobishin slumped lifelessly in his seat.

'This reminds me of something. Is there not a character in a Saltykov-Shchedrin novel who has a clockwork mechanism instead of a brain?'

Oznobishin looked a little shamefaced but did not answer the question.

'First it was Sonya in the Kingdom of Wonder now it is the History of a Town. You are a very literary gentleman, aren't you? In truth, my friend, now I don't know which of your stories to believe, if I can believe any of them.'

'Yesterday I didn't know what I was saying. Begging your pardon, Excellency, I was under the influence.'

'And today you are not?'

'Not so much.'

'Let us stick to the facts, shall we? Rather than fantastical tales. When Sergeant Petrov and I spoke to you yesterday, there was no blood on your clothes at all. If you had committed this crime, shouldn't there have been blood all over you? You were wearing this very coat, I believe. It is quite grubby, but there is no blood on

43

it.'

'I was wearing my apron over it.'

'What apron?'

'I have an apron. For my work.'

'And you took your apron to Tavrichesky Garden yesterday? You were not working then, I think?'

Oznobishin hung his head. He mumbled something that Virginsky did not catch.

'What's that you say?'

'Things have not been going well for me in my business, your Excellency.'

'Perhaps your weakness for the bottle has something to do with that, my friend?'

Oznobishin shook his head sadly, more in regret than denial. He made an appeal to Virginsky's sympathetic nature with a dewy-eyed smile.

'Do you still have this apron?'

'I do.'

'You didn't think to bring it with you?'

'I can fetch it now if you like?'

'We will send an officer to get it. Our men will search your premises thoroughly, you need not fear. Perhaps you could tell us what weapon you used to kill the general.'

'My sabre.'

'You have a sabre?'

'I was once in the army.'

'As an officer?'

'I was a *feldwebel*.'

'Did you ever serve under General Krolikov?'

Oznobishin's gaze became distant. 'I have said enough.'

'No, my friend, I will decide when you have said enough. We are only just getting going. Answer the question!' Virginsky slapped his hand down on Petrov's desk for emphasis.

'I killed him. I confess it. Isn't that enough?'

Oznobishin's refusal to answer Virginsky's question told the magistrate everything he needed to know. 'What were you doing in Tavrichesky Garden yesterday?'

'I went to kill that man. The man with the clockwork brain.'

'How did you know he would be there?'

Oznobishin tapped the side of his head again. 'I could hear it, ticking and whirring. It was incessant. I could hear it wherever I was. Now, at least, I have peace.'

'What did you do with his head?'

Oznobishin seemed delighted by the question. 'What would you have me do with it?'

'And what about your sabre? Where did you put that after you had killed him?'

'I saw a man swallow a sword once.' Oznobishin threw this out for serious consideration.

At that point, Zamyotov came up to Virginsky and handed him a telegram. 'This came from Dr Schloss.'

Virginsky looked down at Schloss's response, in which he clarified his measurements. According to the doctor's estimates, the height of Krolikov's killer ranged from 1.5 to 1.7 metres, that is to say, from five *futa* to five *futa* and seven *dyuma.*

'Stand up.'

Oznobishin was taken aback by the command. After looking uncertainly towards Petrov, he eventually complied.

'How tall are you?'

Oznobishin shrugged.

'Six *futa*?'

'A little over.'

If Schloss was right, Oznobishin was clearly not the killer. But something connected him to Krolikov.

'Who brought you here this morning?'

'What do you mean?'

'You were here bright and early, and yet, as you have admitted, you had a heavy day of it yesterday.'

'It played on my conscience. I couldn't get any peace until I had confessed.' Oznobishin's tone was wheedling. He was pleading with Virginsky to believe him, almost as if life depended on it. That didn't make it true.

Virginsky thought for a moment, considering what to do with the man. On balance, he decided that he would learn more with

Oznobishin at liberty. 'You may go.'

Oznobishin was stunned. 'But I killed him! Because of his clockwork head!'

Virginsky waved the tradesman away. Finally, reluctantly, Oznobishin tore himself away from Petrov's desk. He staggered across the room, though the unsteadiness of his walk seemed to be less from inebriation than the impact of some powerful emotion. Shock, perhaps. Or fear.

As Virginsky watched, something seemed to come over Oznobishin. His body tensed and stiffened. He threw back his head and let out an animal roar, then rushed at a uniformed officer who was coming in the other direction. The startled policeman, a grey-whiskered fellow close to pensionable age, stopped in his tracks and leant so sharply backwards he nearly fell over. Oznobishin threw out a hand towards the uniform's head as if he was going to strike him. But instead he snatched away the man's kepi, dashed it onto the floor and stamped on it repeatedly with his right foot, as if it was a poisonous snake he was determined to kill. Perhaps he thought it was.

Then Oznobishin broke off from his energetic stomping and fumbled at his trouser buttons, before relieving himself with a noisy trickle into the already insulted and abused cap.

Up until this point, it seemed that everyone watching had been too stunned to intervene. But now half a dozen of the assaulted officer's comrades rushed at the offender and wrestled him to the ground. They were understandably enraged by the disrespect shown to one of their own, and let their feeling be known by the harshness of their threats and the zeal of their fists.

Sergeant Petrov bolted over to restore order, hauling men up by the collars as he shouted at them to lay off. Virginsky followed, his interest piqued. Oznobishin lay bloody-faced on the ground, writhing and groaning with his eyes winced closed as he clutched his stomach in pain. His attackers must have landed a fair number of kicks and punches before the sergeant called them to order.

Oznobishin's shoulders began to quake. Virginsky was afraid he was about to have some kind of seizure. You could never tell with these unstable types, especially the drinkers. But no. It was not

46

that. It was simply that he was laughing.

'Get this lunatic into a cell!' ordered Petrov. 'And don't lay a finger on him. Can't you see, he's not right in the head?' For good measure, he clipped one of the chastened officers around the ear.

Virginsky watched as Oznobishin was manhandled away, his feet dragging, his body limp and surrendered, apart from the occasional shaking of his laughter.

11

Oznobishin was charged with assaulting an officer and damaging Imperial property. Despite his arrest, he remained in good spirits for at least the next hour or so. He seemed to find everything that happened to him amusing. He chuckled when the laces were taken out of his boots and his pockets emptied of coins. He giggled when he was forced to surrender a near-empty bottle of vodka from the depths of his overcoat. And when the police cell door was slammed to behind him, he collapsed into a fit of uncontrollable belly laughs.

When he wasn't laughing, he sang. He possessed a decent bass voice and favoured maudlin drinking songs, which brought tears to his eyes while he was singing them, though afterwards he slapped his thighs and whooped with delight as he sat on the edge of the wooden board that served as a bunk.

After an hour, his tuneful ebullience deserted him. He slumped against the wall of his cell and let out a low, sustained moan, which periodically rose to a mournful keening. This naturally grated on the nerves of the custody officer, who from time to time shouted to him to be quiet.

During the next phase of his confinement, he begged for the bottle to be returned to him. 'Just a snifter, sir! One sip will do me! I just need to wet my lips. They's sticking to my gums, you see. And my head, sir. The inside of my head is filled with metal wasps. Their wings are viciously sharp, sir, you wouldn't believe it. Just a sniff of the flask would see me right. I beg you, sir, as a humane gentleman, to unstop the bottle and hold it before this hatch so that I may breathe in the spiritous fumes. I will not trouble you anymore. I swear to you, on my mother's grave, and my children's lives. Just do this one small favour for me, sir, and you will not hear another peep out of me. If it cannot be vodka - perhaps there are rules, I don't know - then may I trouble you for a small glass of wine, or even kvass? I will not even turn my nose up at beer. It is medicinal, sir, in my case. You see. If I do not have my dose of alcohol, I will die. I have been told this by an eminent doctor. I was issued with a certificate that says as much, although I have sadly mislaid it. Look at me, man! I'm drenched in sweat!'

At this point, his teeth began to clatter violently together.

'You see how it t-t-t-takes me, sir. It is the c-c-c-cold sweats. I am d-d-drenched in sweat and yet inside, inside, I am as c-c-c-cold as the Siberian wastes.'

Next came the hysterical screaming. He batted the air frantically, to ward off some imagined pest that was plaguing him, perhaps the metal wasps after they had burst out of his head.

For reasons known only to himself, he stripped naked, tearing his clothes off as if they had combusted. Then he lay down in an embryonic posture, his face to the wall, his curved back overhanging the edge of his bunk. Before long, another fit of shivering came over him, so violent that at times his body lifted from the board. Eventually, he was driven to use his overcoat as a blanket, pulling it up over his head. Then, at last, to the relief of the custody officer, he fell asleep, though his snores reverberated throughout the basement.

Soon it was dinnertime. Oznobishin woke when the hatch in his cell door was yanked open and a tin bowl of broth was shoved through. By now full-blown delirium tremens had settled in. He shook so much that he spilled most of his meal.

The first part of the afternoon was spent weeping. When he could weep no more, he howled obscene curses at the long-suffering custody officer.

12

Virginsky squinted against the flaring sun.

He was standing in front of a large, single-storey warehouse on Kuznechny Lane. Gradually his eyes adjusted to the light conditions and the details of the building emerged. He saw that it was a crude wooden construction, which was either painted black or blackened with grime. The building had a neglected air that fitted precisely with his preconception of what the business premises of a drunkard would look like. He angled his head to read out the letters of a hand-written sign that had been propped up perpendicular to the ground: 'OSIP'S FODDER.' The sign had clearly fallen down from a more prominent position higher up.

Next to him, Sergeant Petrov wielded a large crowbar as if he were impatient to do violence to something, or someone.

'Do you think you can get inside?' asked Virginsky. He quickly added the qualification: 'Without causing too much damage?'

Petrov grunted and strode forwards like a boxer thrusting out of his corner. There were two entrances: a single door with a cracked glass panel in it, which presumably led to Oznobishin's office; and a large double door for carts to pass through. Petrov set to work on the padlock that held the double doors together. It was a matter of seconds before the lock flew off and clattered to the ground.

The man had his uses, Virginsky supposed.

One of the big doors creaked open outwards under Petrov's teasing, then fell slightly on its rusty hinge. The ragged bottom scraped along the ground before jamming against it. The gap between the two doors was just wide enough for a man to squeeze through.

Petrov threw Virginsky a complicated glance, both shamefaced and defiant. He slipped through to the other side noiselessly.

Virginsky yanked at the partly opened door, pulling it off the last bolt that was holding it in place. Virginsky's hand was twisted over as the heavy wooden sheet succumbed to gravity and wrenched itself out of his grip. The door crashed to the ground, throwing up a cloud of black dust. He was left dazed and deafened, as if in the aftermath of an explosion.

A few passers-by quickened their step to distance themselves from the catastrophe. Virginsky didn't look too closely at them, but he had the impression that they were peasants from the countryside. Moskovskaya District was one of the areas of St Petersburg that attracted migrant workers from the outlying villages. There was a chance they thought he was up to no good, but he didn't think they would cause any trouble. They were not the sort of people to go to the local police station voluntarily. Of course, he had a legitimate reason for being there. It would just be inconvenient to have to explain why he had not involved the Moskovskaya District police in his inquiry.

Petrov reappeared in the sudden opening to survey the damage, a barely suppressed grin in place. 'I didn't do that,' he pointed out. 'You did that.' His second observation was even more redundant than the first.

'The place is falling down,' Virginsky observed calmly.

His footsteps sounded on the stone floor, as he stepped into the echoing darkness of the warehouse. All around him he heard a soft rustling and the sough of collapse, like a mass exhalation. He felt his skin crawl, instinctively. The air was cold and damp and carried a fetid stench, like something had been left to rot. In his experience, such a smell was never a good omen. It invariably presaged the discovery of corpses.

But in this case, he suspected the corpse in question was that of a defunct business. It was Oznobishin's product that had turned rotten, and the stirring he had heard was caused by the scuttling away of vermin frightened by the noise of his entrance and the sudden intrusion of sunlight.

Virginsky left Petrov to look around the loading bay and storage bins and made his way into the office, a partitioned-off area in one corner of the warehouse.

The small room was cramped and cluttered, the floor strewn with litter. An empty bottle rolled away as his toe inadvertently kicked against it. A camp bed was pushed against one wall, suggesting that this was where Oznobishin lived as well as worked. The remnants of a meal left out on the desk confirmed it.

The desk itself was an imposing affair that took up much of the available space. Virginsky interpreted it as the hangover from a more prosperous and optimistic time in the business's fortunes. It was currently buried under mounds of paperwork and ledgers.

Virginsky scanned the chaos and noticed invoices and receipts dating back months and years. Nothing recent caught his eye. It would all need to be boxed up and taken back to the station so that he could work through it, looking for the connections that Oznobishin refused to disclose.

That was a job for another time. Now his priority was to find the weapon and apron that would corroborate, or disprove, Oznobishin's story. No doubt some would think him excessively scrupulous in not simply accepting the word of a mentally deranged alcoholic. After all, why would the man confess to the crime if he hadn't done it? But Virginsky knew that false confessions were common, more common than most people realised. He also knew that they could throw an investigation off track for days.

What motivated these eccentrics was different in every case, of course. Most often, it boiled down to a desire for attention. The people who came forward falsely claiming to be murderers were invariably sad, lonely individuals, who felt overlooked and powerless in their lives. For a brief moment, they were at the centre of things. They had policemen and magistrates hanging on their every word.

Virginsky did not think this was the case with Oznobishin. Nor did he believe that it was simply because the man was deluded. There was something going on here. If Oznobishin was not General Krolikov's murderer, he had a very good reason for pretending to be.

It was not unheard of for a false confession to be made in order to shield the real perpetrator. Perhaps that was behind Oznobishin's claims. But somehow Virginsky doubted it.

Virginsky stood on a spot as near to the centre of the office as he could and slowly rotated, to take in the whole room. The door from the main warehouse was open. Virginsky pushed it to. There hanging on the back of it was a light-coloured apron. Virginsky lifted it from its hook and held it open to examine it. The front was smeared with rust-coloured stains.

Blood?

He would leave that for Dr Schloss to determine.

For the time being, Virginsky placed the apron back on its hook while he continued searching. First he crossed to the back of the desk and pulled out the drawers one by one. They were mostly crammed full of more papers. But the last drawer he opened released a buzzing cloud of flies and an intensification of the fetid smell he had experienced when he first set foot in the warehouse.

A small parcel wrapped in soggy newspaper sat unmistakably in a coagulated pool of blood. He gingerly peeled the paper apart to reveal a lump of something that had come from a butcher's shop, though not recently. There was a strong tang of iron in the smell. The object, Virginsky guessed, was a liver.

Something else for Dr Schloss to get to the bottom of.

Footsteps announced Petrov at the doorway. Virginsky looked up to see the sergeant holding a sword out in front of him, his arms outstretched, the curved scabbard resting on both of his palms as if he were making an offering of it.

13

Virginsky was back at the station soon after three. He left Petrov to organise the retrieval of documents from Oznobishin's office, giving instructions for the apron and liver to be sent to Dr Schloss. All that would have meant liaising with the nearest Moskovskaya District police station, and Virginsky had no desire to get bogged down in the bureaucratic niceties that would entail.

He quietly took command of the sword himself, on the grounds that it was a matter of some urgency that he establish the principal plank of Oznobishin's confession: that he had chopped General Krolikov's head off with his old army sabre.

With the door to his office securely closed, he drew the weapon from its scabbard. The blade was a little sluggish coming out, ruining the self-conscious flourish he attempted. He held it up to the window to examine it. The steel was dull, in places blooming with oxidation. It was this corrosion that had snagged as he had tried to cut a figure with it. It clearly hadn't been unsheathed for years.

The shape of the blade was consistent with Oznobishin's description of it as a sabre. But it seemed unlikely that this antique had chopped off anyone's head recently.

Virginsky placed the blade down on his desk and examined the mottled steel more closely through a magnifying glass. The cutting edge was as dull as the rest of the steel. He doubted it had seen a whetstone in a long time. He pressed against it with his thumb then turned the pad towards him. There was no blood drawn. He was merely left with a rusty indentation.

As far as he could tell - though it would be left to Dr Schloss to confirm it for certain - there was no trace of anything that could be blood on the blade.

It was time to have another chat with Oznobishin.

*

The shutter was closed over the hatch in the cell door, but

Oznobishin's cries were distinctly audible.

Virginsky gave the officer a sympathetic nod. 'How long has he been like this?'

'Like what?'

Virginsky gestured towards the cell. 'So vociferous.'

'Oh, you get used to it, your Honour. I scarcely notice it now.'

Virginsky snorted at the man's blatant lie. He wondered if there was any point trying to talk to Oznobishin while he was in this state. Perhaps a full day and a night in the cells would calm him down. 'Has he eaten anything?'

'We gave him his dinner. But it's booze he wants.' The officer lifted Oznobishin's vodka bottle from beneath his counter.

'Give me that, will you.'

The officer's eyes widened with surprise but he handed the bottle over. Virginsky sauntered over to the cell door and opened the hatch. Peering in, he was taken aback to see that Oznobishin was naked.

'Good God, man. Put something on, will you? I can't talk to you like that.'

Perhaps it was the shock of seeing the magistrate on the other side of his cell door, but Oznobishin grew meekly compliant. He hurried to cover himself in his overcoat.

Virginsky lifted the bottle so that Oznobishin could see it. 'Is this what you want?'

'Oh, your Excellency! You are my saviour!' Oznobishin reached towards the open hatch, his hands clenched into grasping claws.

Virginsky snatched the bottle away. 'You can have it, but you have to give me something first.'

'Anything, your Excellency!'

'What is your relationship to General Krolikov?'

Oznobishin's expression underwent several rapid transformations, before settling on a look of pathetic cunning. 'General Krolikov, you say?'

'You know him.' It was not a question. 'In Tavrichesky Garden, you called him the White Rabbit, even before we had told you his name was Krolikov.'

'I had the honour to serve under the general in the Caucasus, back in '64. Even then, he had a shock of snowy white hair. I was a humble *feldwebel,* working in supplies. And yet I do not flatter myself if I say that the general noticed me. An army marches on its stomach. That was one of his great sayings. But what he did not say, which is also true, is that the stomachs of its horses are equally important. Or perhaps the stomach of an army includes the stomachs of its horses? I will leave that for greater minds than mine to unravel.'

'When was the last time you were in contact with the general? Before his death yesterday, I mean.'

'It was many years ago. Back in the sixties, as I said. In Sochi, it was. I remember it well, the snow lay fresh upon the ground. The road was thick with...' Oznobishin broke off, his eyes moist with private emotion. He shook his head violently, as if to dispel the unwanted memory. 'But it was all so long ago now. Why go into that?'

'No. You have seen him more recently than that, I am sure of it.'

Oznobishin struck himself forcefully on the chest. 'I swear to you, your Excellency, on all that is holy, I swear I had not seen him since the old days, until...'

'Until what? Do you still insist that you killed him?'

Oznobishin's expression grew comically abashed. 'I may have been mistaken about that. I often get confused.'

'You can't possibly have killed him, my friend. For one thing, you're too tall. For another, that sabre of yours is so blunt it couldn't cut through air. So the question is, why were you so determined to have us believe that you did?'

'It doesn't matter now.'

'Why? What's changed?'

Oznobishin gave an evasive shrug. 'May I have my vodka now?'

'No. Because you are not being honest with me. Do you really expect me to believe that it was entirely by coincidence that you happened to be in Tavrichesky Garden the same day that your old commander was killed?'

'Coincidences happen.'

'As an investigating magistrate, I'm afraid I have learnt to be very suspicious of coincidences.' Virginsky slammed the hatch shut and returned the bottle to the custody officer.

Oznobishin's cries resumed, his curses more colourful and violent than before. Only now, the object of his hatred was Virginsky.

14

That evening, Virginsky dined alone at Domenika's on Nevsky Prospect. It was a place he used to come to with Porfiry Petrovich. On one memorable occasion, Porfiry and he had been playing billiards. Porfiry was having the worst of the play, but rather than admit defeat and lose the wager, he picked a fight with some obnoxious soldiers, and the two of them were obliged to beat a hasty retreat, furniture, champagne bottles and billiard cues smashing around them.

Virginsky couldn't help smiling to himself at the memory.

Since Porfiry's retirement, Virginsky had for the most part refrained from consulting his former mentor on matters relating to his investigations. In fact, he had rather got into the habit of staying away from Porfiry altogether. He had asked his advice once, recently, and that had not ended well. And so a distance had opened up between them again. The last words that Virginsky had said to Porfiry were harsh and recriminatory. Now, he wondered if they were not also undeserved.

He read a newspaper as he ate, one of those that the restaurant provided, attached to a rod to prevent him from walking off with it. General Krolikov's murder had made it into the late editions.

HORROR AT TAVRICHESKY GARDEN
GENERAL BEHEADED ON HIS NAME DAY
FAMILY DISTRAUGHT
HEAD MISSING

There was a kind of brutal but bathetic poetry to the headlines. But he supposed all the essentials of the case were there. In the article itself, the police - and by extension, the investigating magistrate - were inevitably portrayed as hopeless incompetents. The writer regretted that the great Porfiry Petrovich was no longer available to solve the case, which must be left to lesser talents. He urged those struggling to make sense of this horrific and mysterious crime to call upon the master detective, who, it was suggested, might be employed in the role of a consultant.

Virginsky looked around furtively. The dining room was busy.

THE CRIMSON CHILD

His table was in a far corner, neglected by the waiters, whose attention was commanded by a boisterous party on the other side of the room. Their braying laughter drowned out any other sounds, such as the sound of Virginsky tearing the article from its page.

A quick sweeping glance as he tucked the scrap of paper into an inside pocket reassured him that he had got away with it.

On his way out, Virginsky returned the newspaper to its rack.

Outside, the light was beginning to fade. The white nights of summer were fast approaching, but for now the evening hours were still enfolded in a soft and welcome darkness.

He set off without any clear direction in mind. Certainly, it was not his intention to go straight home to his empty apartment.

He doubted that he would sleep easily tonight and was so delaying the moment that he lay his head against the pillow. First, he wanted to wear himself out walking the streets. It was an old habit, begun in his student days. Virginsky was not a native St Petersburger. His long walks had been a way to assimilate the plan of the city, by imprinting the pattern of its streets on his physical memory.

There was much preying on his mind. Perhaps he hoped to walk some of it off.

Virginsky reckoned himself to be an atheist, a scientific materialist, unlike the unashamedly spiritual Porfiry Petrovich. But he was also a Russian. The concept of a soul proved tenacious. And he felt his soul weighed down, to borrow the terminology that Oznobishin had used.

First, the atrocity of the crime lay as an insult to all notions of man's humanity. When deeds like this were possible, one could only conclude that man was inherently evil.

Then, he had sought - and failed to find - some kind of solace in a reconciliation with Maria Petrovna. What stood between them was his secret guilt. Before they could be reconciled, he had had to confess to that. They say confession is good for the soul. But it had not felt good for Virginsky's. Maria Petrovna had sent him away, his soul even more weighed down.

She had questioned his motives and accused him of emotional subterfuge, or worse, crass manipulation.

He knew now that he must earn his own redemption. He could not borrow hers.

Virginsky could hardly believe that his thinking was framed around words like 'soul' and 'redemption'. If Porfiry Petrovich could hear him, he'd be laughing into his fist. Or perhaps he'd rejoice, believing that at last Virginsky was halfway to saving.

He was suddenly overcome by a powerful desire to see his old friend. By some strange action of his subconscious, his steps had brought him within a block of Porfiry's apartment building.

*

Virginsky was shocked to see how diminished Porfiry Petrovich appeared when he opened the door. The great investigative magistrate had shrunk in every direction, his frame wasted away, his shoulders stooped, even the features of his face so drawn that the shape of his skull could be seen. His skin had grown so pale it appeared translucent. His pale grey eyes, which had once been as bright as sunlight on ice, appeared weak and watery. He barely had the strength to blink.

The energy had gone from him entirely. His head bobbed minutely in acknowledgement of Virginsky's presence. It could hardly be called a greeting. He turned his back on his guest and shuffled away, leaving him to close the door behind him. In his wake he trailed a musky, unwashed smell.

'My goodness, Porfiry Petrovich, are you ill?'

'Ill? No. Just old.' Porfiry's voice was gravelly, his words dredged up from a place deep inside him. The effort set him coughing.

Porfiry seemed to have aged a decade, if not more, since the last time he had seen him. But that was only a matter of months ago. Could his decline have really come on so quickly?

Porfiry led him into a dimly lit room. Even in the gloom, Virginsky sensed the disorder. It fell short of outright squalor but not by much. There was a vodka bottle open on a low table, a single glass empty beside it.

Porfiry fell back into an armchair, closing his eyes as he

surrendered to gravity, as if he were keen to resume the nap that Virginsky had roused him from.

Virginsky took a seat on an artificial leather settee. The fabric was cracked and completely split in places, the stuffing visible through the holes. Unable to look at Porfiry, he focused on a hole the shape of Italy and stared fixedly at it. 'Porfiry Petrovich, I wanted to see you… to be honest, I've wanted to see you for some time…'

Virginsky was interrupted by the clink of glass, as Porfiry poured himself another shot of vodka. He looked up to see the other man proffering him the bottle. 'Want some?'

Virginsky shook his head. 'Porfiry Petrovich, what has happened to you?'

Porfiry met his solicitude with a look of startled indignation. 'What do you mean?'

'I mean this. You. Drinking vodka on your own.'

'I offered you a glass.'

'But this is not your first of the evening, I think.'

'Who do you think you are, to come here, like this! Judging me! How dare you! Let me remind you, sir, I can do what I like in my home. I pay the rent. Not you. In conclusion, I will not be lectured to by you or anyone else. Least of all you. You're a prig, Pavel Pavlovich. That's always been your problem.'

'This is not you, Porfiry Petrovich!'

'On the contrary, this is my life now.' He waved the bottle carelessly, so that the contents slopped over his front. 'This is my friend. This!' He raised the bottle high so that Virginsky would be in no doubt. 'My only friend.'

'You don't mean that.'

'I… do… mean… it.'

'Porfiry!'

'I mean it, I mean it, I mean it!'

'Well, I don't believe you!'

'Why have you come here? Persecuting me and judging me and picking on me. I didn't ask you to come here.'

'I came here because I wanted to apologise.'

'What have you got to apple-chize for?'

61

'The last time we spoke, I said some things I regret.'

Porfiry waved his hand dismissively. Unfortunately, it was the hand holding the bottle, so he spilled even more vodka. He didn't seem to notice or care. 'I don't remember.'

'I'm sure you do, Porfiry Petrovich.'

'Remind me.'

'I'd rather not. I wish that I could unsay them. I have no desire to repeat them.'

'Did you call me a filthy, dirty, drunken drinkard?' The question didn't quite come out as Porfiry had intended. 'A dilty, filty, drinky drunky...' He began to giggle into his sleeve.

'No, it wasn't that.'

'Then what are you worrying about!' Porfiry gave a sly wink. There was something about that wink that aroused Virginsky's suspicions. He saw an inkling of the man that Porfiry used to be, the kind of man who could provoke a barroom brawl to break up a game of billiards that he was losing.

'Porfiry Petrovich?'

'Mm?'

'Is this one of your little tricks?'

Porfiry was suddenly beaming. He sat up straight in his seat, his ice grey eyes twinkling in the glow of the oil lamp. 'Admit it. I got you. Fair and square. Forgive me, Pavel Pavlovich, but I have been so bored since I last saw you.'

'No. No, no, no. This is... you're a terrible man.'

'Ohh! A little bit of harmless fun. You should have seen your face! *This is not you, Porfiry Petrovich!* I'm surprised you didn't get it when I said that bit about the bottle being my only friend. Thought I was laying it on a bit too thick, to be honest.'

Despite his relief that Porfiry was not the lush that he had imagined him to be, Virginsky's mind was not entirely set at ease. The fact remained that Porfiry Petrovich was a shadow of his former self. He gave every appearance of neglecting himself. He managed to revive his energies as he laid claim to his prank, but the effort of doing that seemed to take its toll on him. The temporary light in his eyes dimmed again. He sank back into his armchair, his hilarity now a faint smile on his lips.

Virginsky knew only one way to restore the magistrate's power. He took out the news report and handed it to Porfiry.

Porfiry leant forward to catch the lantern's glimmer from the table. He held the torn paper at various distances until he found his focal length.

'Very interesting, but why have you given me an advertisement for the circus?'

Bewildered, Virginsky snatched back the paper. 'The other side!' he snapped impatiently, thrusting the article back into Porfiry's hands.

'Pity. I thought you were inviting me to see…' Porfiry glanced down to read: 'Lady Satanaya, the Ubykhian wonder…'

'No!'

'It says here she is both Astounding and Beautiful.'

Virginsky gestured impatiently. Porfiry turned the paper over and repeated the rigmarole of getting the words into focus. 'Ah, yes, the general who lost his head. Very careless of him, if you ask me.'

Porfiry read the article, squinting and blinking and breathing heavily. At last he handed it back to Virginsky. 'This newsprint is very smudged, as if it has been handled by more than one reader. The tearing around the article is rough, suggesting it had been ripped out in a hurry. Indeed, why tear it out at all? I wonder why you did not bring me the whole newspaper, if it was yours to bring. I am inclined to think that you tore this out of a public copy, possibly one of those kept at restaurants for solitary diners to read. The time of your call is consistent with you having dined first. The fact that you have come here to see me tonight, in a somewhat sentimental mood, suggests that it was a restaurant that we used to go to together. Perhaps Domenika? Am I right?'

'I see you have not lost your touch, Porfiry Petrovich.'

Porfiry smiled and sat blinking in the half light. He looked, to Virginsky, like a holy innocent.

'I tore it out, you know, to stop people reading all that guff about you.'

'Quite right, Pavel Pavlovich. Quite right.'

15

The two men stayed up into the early hours discussing the case and other matters. The subject of Maria Petrovna arose.

No vodka was consumed, but Porfiry Petrovich made a samovar of tea that was strong and stimulating. By the time Virginsky left, the sky was beginning to leaven, a milky wash seeping in from the East. But there were still inky recesses at street level, doorways and courtyard entrances, where an attacker might be lurking.

The gaslit streets were deserted. Virginsky's footsteps echoed loudly, advertising his solitary presence to anyone looking for an easy victim to rob. Or a toff to decapitate. Virginsky hated to think of himself in those terms, but as an investigating magistrate, he had to accept that criminals would see him as a member of the establishment, and therefore a valid target.

His nerves jangled, his senses tingled. Partially, it was an effect of the tea. It was also the result of the sustained stress that he had been living under for the past few months. The atrocity in Tavrichesky Garden had not helped. Nor had the re-entry of Loris-Melikov into his life.

He saw the darkness stir in one of the doorways. A figure stepped out and moved sharply towards him.

His muscles tensed in readiness for the fight that was surely coming. Virginsky was no street brawler, but when it came down to it, the instinct for self-preservation was strong. If this individual wished him harm, he would do all that he could to resist him.

The man was wearing a soft workman's cap, the peak pulled down to conceal his eyes. To Virginsky's relief, he appeared to be shorter than average height and slightly built. Perhaps he would be able to take him on in a fight, after all. But then he saw the man's hand flash out dangerously towards him.

Virginsky looked down at the rapidly moving hand in dread, expecting to see a gun or a knife there. He was surprised that the man was holding nothing more threatening than a brown envelope. It was the kind used by civil servants, fastened with a loop.

'A mutual friend wishes you to have this.'

Virginsky had the impression that the man was trying to disguise his voice. It sounded lower than was natural to the speaker, and there was something peculiar about the accent that he affected. It was a kind of country bumpkin accent but it suggested no specific area of Russia.

His heart still thrumming violently, Virginsky grasped the envelope. He held it up to the nearest streetlamp only to discover that there was nothing written on it. He was about to open it when the other man stopped him. 'Not here. Look at it when you get home. Our friend trusts that you will know what to do with it.'

'Who is our friend?'

Virginsky thought he detected a smile on the man's face. 'It is enough to know that our friend wishes you well.' He nodded once and then stepped back to dissolve once more into the shadows.

There was definitely something odd about that voice. The man's efforts to disguise it had slipped a little during his longer statements. Virginsky couldn't shake off the sense that he had heard the speaker before.

He pocketed the letter and hurried on.

16

Back at his own apartment, Virginsky found a second letter waiting for him, one that piqued his interest even more sharply than the mysterious communication handed to him by the little man in the cap.

The letter was addressed to P. P. Virginsky. The handwriting sloped neatly, with the individual letters small and well-formed. For some reason, he thought he detected a teacher's hand at work, and a female teacher at that. His heart pounded almost as hard as it had when he had seen the man come at him from the shadows. The letter could only be from Maria Petrovna.

He tore it open eagerly.

My dearest Pavel Pavlovich,

Please forgive me for my outburst this afternoon. The news you bore hurt me, but it was not your fault and I was wrong to "shoot the messenger". I said things I shouldn't have. I accused you of things that aren't true. My emotions were raw in the wake of your revelations. My heart already broken, was shattered anew.

My initial joy at seeing you was dashed by the devastating information you disclosed. It is hard for me to come to terms with the reality of who my father was. I told you that he came to see me shortly before he took his own life. He was so sweet that day, he reminded me of the father he had been to me when I was a child. Of how he used to sit me on his lap and sing to me. And how my tiny fingers would reach up and play with the whiskers of his moustache.

The bond that is formed between a father and daughter during childhood cannot be broken without intense pain, no matter what the rational, objective facts are concerning those involved.

The things you told me about my father made me hate you. But I realise now that you were only telling me the truth. He was not the man I believed him to be. In recent years, indeed since I have reached adulthood, he and I have not agreed on matters of politics. But there has always been a mutual love and respect there. I always believed him to be a man of honour.

What you said implied that he was not, and I could not bear it. You ripped away the last shred of connection between my father and me. In the moment, I could not forgive you. But now I find that I can. Indeed, that I must. For there was no harm intended on your part.

If I was to hate anyone, it should have been him. But I cannot do that, so I turned my anger on you.

I impugned your motives. I was wrong to do so.

After your visit, I spoke to my mother. We have both agreed that if it is necessary for you to examine my father's private papers, you have our permission to do so.

Yours in sorrow and friendship,

Masha.

Virginsky sighed. Although he could not have asked for more from the letter, it left him troubled.

But there were words in there that he clung to. Her admission of joy at seeing him. Her undoubted candour. Her profession of friendship. The use of the diminutive.

These gave him hope.

He turned his attention to the other letter.

Inside the official-looking envelope he found a letter. The wax seal had been opened but was still attached. It bore an imprint that he recognised: the double-headed eagle of the Romanov family.

The outer bore a single letter: *K.*

Could this really be what it appeared to be? A letter from Tsar Alexander II to his mistress, Ekaterina Dolgorukova?

My angel,

I love you to madness. The moments when we are together are all that I live for. Our love is the water I thirst for. The air that I breathe. The bread that nourishes me. I bask in the sunlight of our love. It saturates me and sustains me. And when I am denied your presence, I am like a starved man. The duties of my position oppress me. You are my only relief, my only happiness. Every moment I am away from you is a life sentence. For I fear that I will never see you again, because the enemies of goodness will take me from you.

But I MUST see you again! I WILL see you again! To live

without that hope is crushing.

Even when, as today, a cloud descends between us.

Was it the customary depression that follows in the wake of ecstasy that upset your mood? I wanted the joy to last for ever. But always there is that fall after a little death into a little hell.

You accused me of I know not what offences. Do you really imagine there is another woman at court who can compete with you for my affections? Is there one whom I could look at and not find wanting, in comparison to your beauty? I will swear to it. There is no one. So why, beloved, do you punish me for crimes that I have not committed? Our time together is brief and precious, I beg you let us not waste it in pets and quarrels.

I know that in your true heart you do not believe the accusation that you made. You feel the same frustration as I and, understandably, it finds outlet in bitter reproaches and petty jealousies.

You are unhappy. You punish me, whom you see as the source of your unhappiness, because I will not give up my destiny for you. No, I will not. I admit it. But that is not because I do not love you. On the contrary, it is because I DO love you! It is because I want my destiny to be your destiny. If I give up everything now so that I may have you, then I will be beggaring you. For one day, all that is mine, all that I am, WILL be yours, my dearest love. I will not surrender it willingly before that day.

And really... really... REALLY! Do you really look on me as the author of your unhappiness? Please tell me it is not so. I am in despair at the thought. Do you really believe that I would knowingly, willingly, purposely do anything that causes you even the smallest degree of suffering? I want only to be a source of joy and happiness to you. You must know that. Tell me that you believe that. My life depends on it.

I beg you, my beloved, have patience. You are my true wife, my wife before God. You are the Empress of my Heart. When the one that stands in the way of our happiness is gone, you will be my wife indeed. And I will make you Empress of Russia.

We do not have long to wait, I am sure of it.

On a happier note, I must tell you what a delight it was for me to spend some time in little Gogo's company this afternoon. He is growing up so quickly! One thing, if you will allow me, my dear - we must not let him have his way in everything. Believe me when I say that he is as precious to me as he is to you, but if we indulge his every whim, there is a danger we will spoil him. I say that as a warning to myself as much as to you, beloved, for how can one not wish to give his precious heart whatever it desires.

But fear not, my darlingest. Thoughts and plans have been forming in my mind! In the sunlit future we both look forward to, the prospect will be very different. Our little Gogo is so dear to me because he is the first product of OUR love. There is nothing that I would not do for him. He is such a good, sweet, loving child! That is why we want to spoil him, because he is so good! One day, I promise you, he will get everything that he deserves.

When I compare him to his brother, the Tsarevich Alexander, it is a source of great regret to me that Gogo will not be my heir. Not as the law stands. But believe me when I say I see him as my true heir - as you are my true wife. Before God, if not in law. Oh, Sasha is not a bad boy. But he has come under the influence of evil men, who are plaiting ropes out of him. He plots against me, or at best looks through his fingers while others do. He is in an ungodly hurry to ascend the throne. He may at least do me the courtesy of waiting till I have vacated it, though I fear he would hasten that day forward.

Gogo is OUR son and so he must be my preferred heir, all things being equal (which alas! they are not). Imagine! A Tsar with undiluted Russian blood! As you know, Sasha has his mother's German blood in his veins.

Perhaps I have said too much. Guard this letter well, angel of my heart. Better still, destroy it.

The letter was not signed. But, if genuine, there could be no doubt who the writer was.

17

By the time Virginsky made it into the station the following morning, the day was under way. He had the sense that something had happened in his absence. An air of chastened excitement had settled over the police department. Uniformed officers clustered for urgent, whispered conferences, watching him warily as he passed them. Others studiously avoided his gaze.

Sergeant Petrov sought him out soon after he had arrived. 'Have you heard?'

'Heard what?'

'Oznobishin.'

'What about him?' But Virginsky had an ominous premonition even as he was asking the question. Not that he believed in ominous premonitions. He left that sort of thing to Porfiry Petrovich. In truth, there was nothing supernatural about it. He could read Petrov's expression easily enough, which was somewhere between a whipped dog and a bereft child.

'He died. Overnight. In his cell. Dr Schloss has examined him, and uh... well, it is unfortunate that he sustained some minor cuts and bruises in that unfortunate rumpus that occurred yesterday. A couple of cracked ribs. It complicates things, no doubt. The doctor cannot be persuaded to exclude those details from his report.'

Virginsky gripped the edge of his desk. 'Nor should he!'

'There will be a full autopsy, of course. There may have been some internal bleeding, we don't know. But that's not what killed him. The doctor is sure of it.'

'Then what did?'

'He appears to have had some kind of epileptic seizure in his cell. Probably brought on by alcohol withdrawal.'

Virginsky's grip on his desk tightened. He gasped a denial. *'No!'*

Petrov was quick to reassure him. 'There's nothing to worry about. It will be put down to natural causes. It was too much for a man of his habits to be denied the bottle so abruptly and completely. It is unfortunate, but there's nothing anyone could have done.'

Virginsky let go of his desk and covered his face with his hands as he groaned. 'I refused him a drink.'

'And you were right to do so. We can't allow a prisoner access to alcohol. There are regulations to be adhered to.'

'But it might have saved his life!'

Petrov shook his head. The matter was straightforward as far as he was concerned. 'He brought this on himself. It was his dissolute way of life that killed him. You bear no responsibility.'

'But it was a matter of common humanity. Besides, I wanted him alive. For the case. There were questions I needed to put to him.'

Petrov looked down, his expression grimly resolute. 'Perhaps it is better this way.'

There was a knock at Virginsky's door. The door opened a crack and Zamyotov peered round, his expression unusually sombre - apprehensive even, Virginsky might have said. 'It is the prokuror to see you.'

'Liputin?' Virginsky sat up. This was all he needed. 'Very well, ask him to come in.' He gave Petrov a curt bow and watched him out of the room.

Virginsky had not seen Liputin since the day of Krolikov's murder, when the prokuror's usual haughtiness had been somewhat overshadowed by the arrival of Count Loris-Melikov.

He strode into the room now, with his head held at a supercilious angle. He carried his dignity stiffly and glared down at Virginsky. He had the air of a man who felt himself slighted and was intent on redress. It seemed he was determined to reassert his authority.

'Your Excellency, please…' Virginsky gestured to the chair on the other side of his desk.

Liputin ignored the invitation. It was clearly not for the likes of Virginsky to tell him when to sit and where. 'I am not here on a social visit. I have come to talk about the Krolikov murder. I understand you have a suspect?'

Virginsky's face must have betrayed the turn the case had taken.

'What is it? Don't tell me you let him go?'

'No. We still have him.'

'Well then?'

'He's dead.'

Liputin's body seemed to grow as he took in this news. His spine straightened and his head tilted upright.

Virginsky went on: 'I am told he suffered some kind of epileptic fit while confined in his cell.'

Liputin's eyes narrowed. 'But he confessed to the crime before he died?'

'Yes, but...'

'This is perfect. And so the case is closed. I congratulate you, Pavel Pavlovich. All the more so as the state will be spared the expense of a long trial of which the outcome is uncertain.'

'Ah but there is a problem.'

'What possible problem could there be?'

'I don't believe he did it.'

'What you believe is of no importance to me. Or to anyone. You will write up a report concluding the case, naming this dead man as General Krolikov's assassin. I shall expect it on my desk first thing tomorrow morning.'

'But if that means Krolikov's true assassin remains free to kill again?'

'Don't be ridiculous, Pavel Pavlovich. How can he kill again if he is dead in a police cell?'

'But I must insist, Oznobishin is not the killer. Dr Schloss has calculated...'

'Calculated? Your doubts rest on calculations?' Liputin shook his head dismissively. 'I do not believe in calculations.'

'Not only that...'

'A confession trumps a calculation. Juries are confused by calculations. But they understand confessions. However, we are fortunate in that this need not go to a jury. You will construct a case proving that this man Oznobishin is the general's killer. There is no need to include Dr Schloss's calculations. The confession will suffice. And any other incriminating evidence you may have. Have you found the weapon, by chance?'

'There was a sword found at Oznobishin's warehouse...'

'Excellent!'

'But I do not...'

'I'm not interested in what you do not. You need not seek any other suspect in connection with this horrible crime. The news will come as a tremendous relief to the people of St Petersburg, who for the last day or so have been living under the shadow of an unendurable terror. I venture to say that you will earn the Tsar's gratitude by your swift and decisive action.'

Virginsky was beginning to think that the Tsar's gratitude was something he could live without.

'I do not rule out the possibility of an honour of some kind. Just ensure that your report says what it needs to say. Good day, Pavel Pavlovich.'

Liputin swept from the room, taking his dignity with him.

18

Later that morning, two boxes were deposited on the floor of Virginsky's office by a couple of uniformed police. They contained the papers and accounts books from Oznobishin's office. Given that Liputin had declared the case closed, there was arguably no good reason for Virginsky to look through the boxes now. But the prokuror had wanted a report, had he not? Perhaps there was something in here that could inform Virginsky's findings.

He began with the order book.

As he had gathered when he had scanned the debris on Oznobishin's desk, it appeared that the business had not been trading for some time. The most recent order entered was for six months earlier, but whether it had been fulfilled was unclear. There was no sign of any invoice or receipt relating to it.

Virginsky looked back through the names of Oznobishin's customers. It wasn't long before he found what he was looking for. The name Krolikov recurred at regular intervals, going back to the start of the current book. He rooted out the previous order book and found Krolikov's name throughout that too.

So, not only had Oznobishin served under Krolikov in the Caucasus, the general was a customer of his. That made sense. The former commanding officer would have done what he could to support his veterans as they tried to make their way in civilian life.

Or perhaps there was more to it than that. Perhaps Oznobishin had some kind of hold over the general, forcing Krolikov to patronise Oznobishin's business?

Virginsky had to say that until the sudden break in record keeping, Oznobishin's accounts were in good order. The business seemed to have been run efficiently, and while it did not bring in a fortune, it was ticking over. The decline appeared abrupt.

The last ever entry in the order book was for the Ciniselli Brothers' circus, dated November 19th, 1879. The Cinisellis had been another regular customer of Oznobishin's up to this point, although as you would expect their order had far exceeded General

Krolikov's.

If the case were still open, he would almost certainly be considering a visit to the circus. But it was not, and so if he were to go, it could only be as a private citizen seeking entertainment. Virginsky did not rule out that possibility. Perhaps, he thought idly, he would invite Maria Petrovna to accompany him, given the promise of reconciliation that her letter had held out.

Similarly, Virginsky ought to have had no interest in Dr Schloss's report on the apron and piece of offal found at the warehouse. He read it, all the same.

Schloss confirmed that the stains on the apron were blood. However, the pattern was not consistent with arterial spray, as he would have expected if the marks had got there when when Krolikov was decapitated. The stains could more accurately be described as smears than spray or spatter. In Schloss's opinion, they had been caused by someone rubbing a blood-soaked object against the apron. He noted the presence of microscopic particles on the surface of the cloth. This brought him onto the organic matter wrapped in newspaper, which he identified as a sheep's liver. He was reasonably confident that the particles on the apron had come from this liver.

As a footnote, Schloss added that he found no trace of blood on Oznobishin's sabre.

To Virginsky, all this was further evidence of Oznobishin's innocence. But also of his desperation.

Virginsky interpreted the bloodstains on the apron as the merchant's ham-fisted attempt to manufacture evidence against himself. Or perhaps it was not so ham-fisted after all. Maybe he wanted to plant just enough circumstantial evidence to arouse suspicion against him, but to do it so ineptly that he would never be convicted. Any half-decent defence lawyer would have a murder charge laughed out of court.

It was a dangerous game. But why was Oznobishin so desperate to have them believe him Krolikov's murderer?

At first Virginsky had thought that someone must have put pressure on him. He came to the station early yesterday morning - earlier than a drunk would normally have been up and about.

Someone must have picked him up and brought him in - or so Virginsky had inferred. He remembered Loris-Melikov telling him that he did not believe it would take him long to solve the case. It was as if he knew something. As if he knew that Oznobishin was going to confess.

And so, he had thought that Loris-Melikov had got to Oznobishin. Perhaps he had even offered him money to make his false confession. But who would confess to a murder they had not committed merely for money?

Virginsky was tempted to answer his own question: only a madman.

But Virginsky did not believe in Oznobishin's madness anymore. Certainly, the merchant had not been as mad as he would have them believe.

Oznobishin confessed to a crime that he obviously didn't commit, and half-heartedly manufactured evidence to back up that confession. But no jury would have ever found him guilty, even if Virginsky had pursued the charge. At the very worst, Oznobishin would have been confined to a lunatic asylum, from where, provided he was able to convince the doctors he was cured, he might someday have secured his release.

Virginsky did not now believe that Loris-Melikov was behind Oznobishin's confession. Indeed, he had to get out of the habit of seeing him behind everything.

There was only one man responsible for Oznobishin's confession and that was Oznobishin himself. He wanted them to arrest him. He didn't care for what. That's why he whipped off the policeman's *kepi* and urinated into it.

He was not acting like a madman. He was following a very rational plan, if you accepted that the purpose of his plan was to get himself arrested.

The question then was why?

There was only one answer Virginsky could come up. Because Oznobishin was afraid. So afraid he believed himself safer inside a police cell than anywhere else.

*

As the working day came to an end, Virginsky remembered the report that Liputin had ordered him to make. He sighed heavily and drew out a notepad pre-printed with the crest of the Department of Justice.

He began to write, filling the page with all the reasons Oznobishin could not be General Krolikov's killer, including Dr Schloss's calculations about the height of the assassin, the pattern of the bloodstains on the apron suggesting smearing rather than spatter, the bluntness of the supposed murder weapon and the weakness of Oznobishin's confession. Virginsky concluded by recommending further lines of investigation to discover the murderer.

He then wrote a second report, which consisted entirely of one sentence: 'Shortly before his death in custody, the merchant Oznobishin confessed to the murder of General Krolikov, therefore no further investigation is currently being conducted on this case.'

The second report was for Liputin. The first, he would send to Loris-Melikov.

19

That evening he called on Madame Verkhotseva and her daughter at the family's third floor apartment on Bolshaya Morskaya Street. He carried Maria's letter in his inside breast pocket, as if it were his credentials. Did he believe that she would go back on her offer and that he would be required to confront her with her own words?

Perhaps it was more that he did not believe himself forgiven.

Although professionally he'd had dealings with Maria's father, this was the first time he had met the mother.

It was fair to say that Verkhotsev's widow was not what he expected.

He had been guilty of building the major into a figure of abstract menace, a sinister shadow, more demon than man, capable of ruthless acts in the service of a brutal ideology. He had struggled at times to reconcile that image of Verkhotsev with his idea of Maria Petrovna.

The contemptible profession of the father - he had been a major in the secret police for God's sake! - had seemed incompatible with the transparent virtue of the daughter, who had founded a charitable school for child labourers. It made him admire Maria Petrovna all the more. What courage it must have taken for her to stand in defiance of her father! But then again, what goodness too, that she had somehow been able to continue loving him.

Of course, he knew that he placed her on a pedestal. The real Maria Petrovna was more complex than the plaster saint his imagination at times made of her. But the unrealistic polarity he had constructed between Maria and her father demanded it. The blacker he painted Verkhotsev, the more virtuous Maria had to become.

This visit, he realised, was the beginning of the process of correcting his illusions.

It surprised Virginsky - he would almost say it shocked him - to discover that the hated Verkhotsev had a domestic life. That he had a wife who loved him, not - he would say - fiercely, but gently, with sympathy and trust. Such was the impression of the woman who received him.

He would not say she was a great beauty, nor ever had been. It must have been some other quality in her that had captivated Verkhotsev. She was rather short and plump, and gave an impression of homeliness rather than glamour. Not that she was dull, far from it. A keen intelligence shone in Galina Filippovna Verkhotseva's forthright gaze.

Yet there was something else in her demeanour that he could not ignore, a more recent addition, he suspected. It was a kind of angry bewilderment that he recognised as grief. It was there in her eyes, not because they were red with weeping - it seemed she had cried herself past that stage - but because they met him with an uncomprehending but uncompromising glare. He had the sense that she needed answers but did not know how to frame the questions.

There must have been times in the recent weeks and months that she had been overwhelmed by despair. But she had come through it. Virginsky believed that she had done so by accepting it and allowing it to work through her. Naturally, it would have changed her in the process.

The vague apprehension that he had felt at the prospect of his visit sharpened into a precise embarrassment. He had been present when Verkhotsev had shot himself. He knew that Maria Petrovna knew this but was unsure whether Galina Filippovna had been told. Would she want to talk about the details of her husband's death? If so, how could he possibly couch his account?

Worse still, would she in some way blame him? Perhaps she believed that he was one of those who had driven Verkhotsev to his death?

Mother and daughter were dressed in black. Their mood was sombre but not unwelcoming. He was invited to join them at an oval table in a comfortably furnished room. The muted lighting came from wall-mounted gas fittings, and an oil lamp in the middle of the table.

They drank tea together, smiling bravely and sighing with deep feeling. And Virginsky realised that the life that Verkhotsev had made for himself inside this cosy apartment was the wellspring of his actions. He did what he did not because he was evil, but because he saw it as the only way to protect the people whom he loved.

At length, Galina Filippovna placed down her empty glass and turned to Virginsky with a steady, unsmiling gaze. 'I understand you want to look through my husband's private papers.'

'With your permission.'

'Why do you want to do this?'

'I hope to discover something that may help to explain Major Verkhotsev's death.'

'What is there to explain? My husband killed himself. Surely you do not suspect that someone else was involved?'

'It is not so much that. Surely you would like to know why your husband took his own life?'

One eyebrow rose questioningly on the widow's face. '*Why?* Of course. It is a question I have asked myself a thousand times. I fear there can be no satisfactory answer. You must know that he did not leave a note?'

'Yes. That is why we must look a little deeper.'

'But why do you wish to know this? That's what I don't understand? What is it to you why he killed himself?'

Virginsky stole a glance in Maria Petrovna's direction. She was waiting for his answer with a neutrality so scrupulous it almost seemed hostile.

'We believe your husband was part of a political faction working against the emperor. He may have been supplying domestic terrorists with information. His position was compromised and consequently pressure was put on him to... well, no doubt they would phrase it thus: to do the honourable thing.'

'Who is this "they"?'

'That's what I hope to find out.'

'And when you have found it out, what will you do?'

Virginsky hesitated a moment before answering her question, as frankly as he was able. 'I have been ordered to infiltrate the same faction.'

'To what end?'

'To expose them and... hold them to account.'

'Aren't you taking a risk in telling me this? What if I share my husband's political aims and beliefs?'

Virginsky conceded her point with a bow. 'Perhaps you once did. But now I suspect that you are motivated more by a desire to know the truth.'

'Perhaps that is the last thing I want to know.'

'You must have questions that you want answers to? I can help you find those answers.'

'Ah, so you are doing it for me! How kind of you!'

Virginsky looked away from her mocking gaze, abashed.

'Were you investigating Pyotr Afanasevich when he took his life?'

He looked up. Her eyes blazed confrontation. How quickly she had gone from a gentle middle-aged matron to a formidable and even dangerous antagonist. The tables had been turned on him. 'I... an investigation was ongoing.'

'A secret investigation? You were spying on him?'

Virginsky couldn't help thinking that Galina Filippovna would make a skilled interrogator. 'Believe me, no one regrets the tragic denouement of that investigation more than I. I did not see it coming. I could not. I had not grasped the full extent of the hold these people had over Major Verkhotsev. I am truly sorry. More sorry than I can express.'

'And yet you continue to pry.'

Virginsky winced. 'Because the Tsar's enemies continue to plot.'

'So, you are a loyal tsarist, are you?'

'I am an investigating magistrate employed by the Department of Justice. This is my job. If I don't do it, I will not eat.'

'He has installed his mistress in the Winter Palace.'

'Do I have your permission to search Pyotr Afanasevich's study?'

'If I deny it, what will you do? Send some criminal to break in and steal his papers while we are sleeping?'

Virginsky decided that was one question that he did not need to answer.

Galina Filippovna pursed her mouth and nodded her acquiescence.

20

Virginsky didn't know what he was looking for. But as always in these circumstances, he felt that he would recognise it when he saw it.

What he did not expect to find was a slim, privately published edition of poems, the artfully-set words surrounded by expanses of restful white space. The name of the poet was given as P.A. Verkhotsev. The title of the collection was *Autumn Leaves*.

The book was tucked away inside one of the drawers of Verkhotsev's desk. It was, perhaps, the most surprising secret that Verkhotsev had ever kept.

Virginsky wondered if even his wife was aware of its existence.

Of course, with a man like Verkhotsev, there was every possibility that the volume was not what it appeared to be: a simple book of poems. But for now, he took it at face value.

He opened the book at the first poem.

I flex my fingers
And gaze in wonder
At a sudden star.
The veins bulge
Beneath the skin.
I am veins and limbs
And blood within.
I fold my fingers
Around the broom
And sweep the leaves
Across the sodden ground.
I remember yesterday's yesterday,
When they were green,
And stirring on the heedless tree.
Today, their fallen brethren
Are gathered into bonfire piles.
A slow smouldering begins.
I breathe the smoke
Of a summer gone.
I flex my fingers

And gaze in wonder.

Virginsky took out a notebook of his own and began by writing the first letters of each line, to discover if they formed an acrostic message. When that produced no meaningful phrase, he took the first letter from each poem in the book. But again, nothing came out, not even a name. Perhaps it was the first letter of the first poem, the second letter of the second, the third letter of the third, and so on. No, that didn't work either. So perhaps it was the first letter of the first line from the first poem, followed by the first letter from the second line of the second poem - or should that the second letter…?

He quickly gave up. It was a hopeless task. If the poetry collection truly was a cipher, he needed to find the key that would unlock it.

More promising from Virginsky's point of view was a diary that he found in the same drawer.

Virginsky flicked through the pages. What struck him immediately was that there was nothing written in it apart from certain symbols such as *, †,¶ and §, followed by numbers in the format of a time, for example 19:00.

The entries came to an end in March, around the time of Verkhotsev's death. There was not much to go on, then.

He opened a second drawer and rummaged through its contents until he found the same diary for the previous year, 1879. Again, the only entries consisted of symbols and times, though in this case the entries continued to the end of the year, and the marks were sometimes doubled, for example **, or even tripled, §§§.

He pulled out all the drawers, apart from one, the lowest on the right hand pedestal, which was locked. He was on reasonably good terms with a man who would have no difficulty in forcing the lock, the housebreaker Yevgeny. But Galina Filippovna's earlier jibe deterred him from seeking Yevgeny's help.

The key must be somewhere.

A number of framed photographs were lined up on Verkhotsev's desk. The first showed a younger Galina Filippovna. Her face drew his gaze and held it. The secret was in the eyes, he thought, in a certain playfulness that leavened the dark intensity of the model's enforced stare. A second photograph showed Madame Verkhotseva again, this time with an infant child upon her lap. Virginsky smiled. This was Maria as a baby, dark curls peeping out from a white lace bonnet. She was reaching up towards her mother's face, her right arm slightly blurred as it had been captured in movement.

Virginsky turned the picture over and opened the clips that held the frame in place. As he took the back off, a folded sheet of paper fell out. The sheet contained rows of numbers, followed by one or other of the symbols he had seen in the diaries.

He noticed that the numbers were invariably written in pairs, joined by a hyphen, with each pair separated from the next by an oblique line, or sometimes with a double oblique line. For example, the first line read:

24-19/6-34/32-9//27-80/15-52/8-21/5-99/18-18//30-8/14-72/1-3/2-37/17-7/23-117.*

Here and there were shorter pairings of numbers such as 34-121/11-78, also followed by a symbol.

Virginsky scanned the numbers, looking for patterns to emerge. One thing he noticed was that the first number of the pairings was never higher than 36.

He checked the copy of *Autumn Leaves* again and established that it contained exactly 36 poems. It was a reasonable assumption, therefore, that the first number in each pair always referred to a poem in the collection.

He returned to the first line at the beginning of the diary.

24-19/6-34/32-9//27-80/15-52/8-21/5-99/18-18//30-8/14-72/1-3/1-37/17-7/23-117.*

He then opened *Autumn Leaves* at the twenty fourth poem and counted the letters down to the nineteenth. That gave him the K from *bark*. He wrote it down in his notebook.

The thirty fourth letter of the sixth poem was A, the second A from *alabaster*.

Using the same system, 32-9 produced a P.

He had now spelled out KAP, which was made from the three pairings before the first double oblique line. His first word? Could it be short for Kapitan?

The next cluster of numbers formed what seemed to be a name. RUZOV.

The final grouping resulted in BALLET.

So was each instance of an asterisk in the diaries the record of an appointment with Captain Ruzov at the ballet at whatever time was indicated? Last year's diary was littered with asterisks, and there were six in this year's. It seemed that Major Verkhotsev and this Captain Ruzov were confirmed balletomanes.

But if their enthusiasm for the dance was legitimate, why did Verkhotsev find it necessary to conceal it in a cipher?

Virginsky sat back in Verkhotsev's chair and pondered.

*

Virginsky consulted the clock on the wall. It was approaching midnight. He felt the heat of embarrassment in his face. He had stayed too long, no doubt inconveniencing his hosts. But he had spent a productive evening, deciphering approximately two thirds of the lines of numbers on the sheet of paper. Most consisted of names and places. The shorter ones were harder to understand. One that occurred frequently was AP. He eventually worked out that it stood for Anichkov Palace, and presumably referred to a meeting of the whole faction, or at least its inner cabal.

A group of three letters, POB, caused him difficulty at first, until he realised that it referred to Konstantin Pobedonostsev, the former tutor of the Tsarevich, and a leading reactionary. It did not surprise Virginsky that Verkhotsev had held regular meetings with Pobedonostsev, who was considered to be the leader of the Anichkov Palace faction. Some argued that he was even more important than the Tsarevich, whose interest he promoted. Pobedonostsev was the intellectual and the ideologue of the right. His contempt for the current Tsar was well known.

Virginsky hurriedly put the photograph back in its frame and folded the sheet of numbers into a pocket. Then he gathered up Verkhotsev's diaries, his own notebook and the copy of *Autumn Leaves.*

Maria Petrovna was sitting alone in the room where he had taken tea earlier. She closed the book she was reading and looked up at him. 'My mother has gone to bed,' she told him.

Virginsky winced apologetically. 'I'm sorry. I lost track of time.'

'Did you find what you were looking for?'

'I don't know.' He hesitated, then held her father's poetry collection out to her. 'I found this.'

Her eyebrows shot up with interest as she took hold of the book. Virginsky waited silently as she read the first poem. A smile formed on her lips. She eagerly turned to the next.

'Have you seen it before?'

She did not answer. She was absorbed, could not tear her eyes away from the words.

At last she said: 'May I keep this? I would like to show it to my mother.'

'I'm afraid I need it for my investigation.'

She looked at him sharply. 'This? What has this to do with your investigation? These are his poems. This has nothing to do with… all that.'

'I fear it does.'

'You think you may find out why he killed himself in his poems?'

Virginsky realised that the thought had not occurred to him. 'It's not so much that. The book works as a cipher. It enables me to decode some entries in his diary. I haven't quite finished that work, I'm afraid.'

Maria clutched the book to her chest. 'It is not for you to say whether I may or may not keep this. It is for me to give permission for you to take it.'

'Yes, I understand that.' Virginsky saw that he clearly did not have a right to take the book without the family's consent. 'Of course, I shall leave it with you.'

'I shall show it to my mother tomorrow morning. You may collect it in the afternoon. However, we would like the book back once you have finished with it.'

'Naturally. Thank you.'

Virginsky bowed and took his leave.

21

As soon as he stepped outside the Verkhotsevs' apartment building, Virginsky set off walking, counting his steps as he went.

One… two… three…

This time, he walked to get his thoughts in order.

He had to admit, it was frustrating not to have Verkhotsev's poems. The progress he had made deciphering the numerical chains was stalled. Perhaps he should have spent his time copying the poems into his notebook, so that he didn't need the original. But there was always the chance of mistakes slipping in. Besides, he had been too impatient to see what the hidden messages would reveal.

Eight… nine… ten…

It was clear that Maria Petrovna had never seen the poems before and she seemed to think that her mother hadn't either. But, surely, there must be other copies of the book in existence? If Verkhotsev had used it as a book cipher to communicate with anyone, then at least one other person must have had a copy.

Twenty one… twenty two… twenty three…

An idea was beginning to form in Virginsky's mind. But he was not ready to execute it just yet. First he would have to get the poems back. And there were other details that needed to fall into place too.

Twenty nine… thirty… thirty one…

As always when he was on one of his walks, he paid little conscious attention to his surroundings. That was not the point. He walked to lose himself. His mind was able to split in two. One part of it was focused on counting his steps, the other on working through whatever problem preoccupied him.

Forty…

He did not necessarily expect to solve that problem. It was more that he was able to open up a part of his mind not usually accessible to him. In so doing, he began a process that would lead to a solution.

Forty eight… forty nine… fifty…

Often, he lost all track of time. He frequently found himself on a street he did not recognise in an unfamiliar neighbourhood.

Fifty seven... fifty eight...

That didn't happen now. This time, as his conscious mind re-imposed its grip, he found himself in a familiar enough place: on Nevsky Prospect, standing in front of a confectioner's window. The shop was closed now, but it had recently been fitted with an electricity supply. The owners had installed an illuminated sign, small light bulbs arranged to spell the name of the business, which was kept on at all hours.

Virginsky looked up, wonderingly. It seemed his subconscious mind had led him here.

The shop was called: BALLET'S.

At that moment Virginsky knew what his next move would be.

22

The days grew longer, ending with a slow fade into sudden darkness. The night's stealth always took Virginsky by surprise.

It was the kind of sentiment that Verkhotsev liked to fill his poems with.

After Virginsky had retrieved the book, he didn't return to the apartment on Bolshaya Morskaya Street once. He felt compromised by the operation that he was undertaking, which was essentially to investigate Maria Petrovna's father. It complicated things. There was a strange constraint between them now. He had felt it that evening, in her mother's pointed questioning and her own aggressive neutrality.

Naturally, he wanted to see her again. He thought of her often, and even dreamt of her occasionally. But he had nothing new to tell her.

Instead, he spent a lot of time in Verkhotsev's company. At least that was how it felt as he pored over the major's verses. After he had extracted the secret messages they held, he decided to read them as poems. He wondered whether Verkhotsev had written them to serve as a cipher from the outset. Probably not, he decided. If that was all they were, any random text would have sufficed.

But Verkhotsev had put a great deal of effort into calling forth his nuanced emotional responses and pinning them down with well-honed phrases. That suggested that he had engaged in the activity for its own sake. Whatever else he was, Verkhotsev was a poet.

Virginsky told himself that the verses were not to his taste. They had too much of the whiff of woodsmoke and nostalgia. The metaphors were a little too laboured, he felt. And a wilful obscurity crept in from time to time.

Even so certain images stayed with him. Mostly, the poems were written with a deceptive simplicity. When the meaning did become obscure, he was not alienated by the enigmatic allusions. They worked away at his imagination, sending forth their roots into his subconscious mind. He was content to puzzle away at them, certain that there was a meaning to be discovered, and that the effort of discovering it would be worthwhile.

Politically, he knew that he and Verkhotsev were on opposite sides of the great divide of the day. Virginsky considered himself a liberal. Once, in his student days, he might even have claimed to be a radical. But as he had made his way in his career as a magistrate, he had leant towards a more moderate position. Verkhotsev, on the other hand, had shown himself to be a reactionary. And it had suited Virginsky to turn him into a cartoon villain.

The man's poetry revealed him to be more human and complex than that. No doubt, Verkhotsev's politics informed his poems. But equally you could say that his love of family did too. His conservatism was expressed as a longing for a return to a simpler time, which Virginsky had to admit was painted in attractive colours. It was one step from Verkhotsev's love of hearth and home, from his reverence of native trees and the jams made from their berries, to the kind of militant Slavophilism that bred a rampant xenophobia and an enthusiasm for unbridled tyranny. This was where the desire for a strong Tsar came in.

Verkhotsev was clever enough to keep all this out of his poetry.

But revering the past led you to the view that the present was evil, and all change was to be resisted. It was an easy path to go down, especially if Verkhotsev had swept the leaves from it.

The future was always uncertain. It bred fear as well as hope. The only certainties existed in the past. Paradoxically, the only way forward was to go backwards.

*

The day he chose to act was one of crystalline clarity. The kind of spring day that Verkhotsev looked back to in the third poem in *Autumn Leaves*.

Above the rolling clouds,
A clear infinity of blue.
As the clouds pass,
The light expands

90

To fill the morning.

Virginsky went back to the confectioner's on Nevsky Prospect. This time, the steps that led him there were conscious. And it was late morning, not midnight.

He waited in line to buy a box of chocolates. Then, almost as an afterthought, he handed an envelope to the woman who had served him. 'Oh, would you see that Captain Ruzov gets this, please?'

The woman took the letter as if this were the most natural request in the world. Perhaps there were others who left messages for him?

Virginsky bowed and left the shop.

His thinking was that there had to be a reason why Ruzov and Verkhotsev had met so often in Ballet's.

His play was based on the assumption that Ruzov had a sweet tooth. Of course, it could have been Verkhotsev who determined the venue for their meetings. But he was betting that Ruzov had at least acquired an addiction to the sweet things that were on offer at Ballet's. More than likely, he continued to meet his fellow conspirators there.

Besides, Virginsky had nothing to lose. To anyone who did not have a copy of *Autumn Leaves,* the note inside that envelope was simply a string of incomprehensible numbers.

But if Virginsky was right, Ruzov would be able to decipher his message as an invitation to meet at Ballet's in two weeks' time. As an incentive, Virginsky promised to hand over 'something of great interest to the friends of the true Tsar, the Tsar in waiting.'

Virginsky didn't identify himself in the note. But for ease of recognition, he proposed that they should both come to the meeting carrying a copy of Verkhotsev's poems.

23

The next two weeks dragged. Now that the investigation into Oznobishin's murder had been officially shelved, Virginsky was left with little of substance to occupy himself. His imagination filled the gap by constructing catastrophic scenarios of how his scheme to infiltrate the Anichkov Palace faction might play out. Agonising as the wait was, such a long interval was necessary to give Ruzov and his cronies the opportunity to receive and process his overture.

Eventually, the time came for him to present himself at Ballet's. His vague anxieties were replaced by frightening realisation: what he was about to do was extremely dangerous. It might even result in his death. He almost hoped that Ruzov hadn't received his message, or if he had, that he chose to ignore it as the work of a crank. It was not to be.

As he walked into the confectionary shop to keep his appointment, he could tell which one was Captain Ruzov even before he saw the copy of *Autumn Leaves* on the table in front of him.

The man was wearing the uniform of an officer of the Hussars, with gleaming boots and sword scabbarded at his side. He maintained the stiff, upright posture of a martinet, even while seated.

Ruzov looked up as Virginsky approached his table, his own copy of the poetry book half-concealed by the arm that held it against his body. Ruzov's face bulged with indignation, as if he regarded Virginsky's presence as a great imposition.

'Who the devil are you?' he demanded as soon as Virginsky was seated.

'My name is Pavel Pavlovich Virginsky. I am a magistrate.' Virginsky could have given a false name, but he believed it was better to keep as much truth as possible in whatever he told Ruzov. That way he was less likely to get caught out in a lie. 'But all that really matters is that I am sympathetic to your cause.'

'How do you know anything about my cause?'

'I served with Major Verkhotsev at the Third Section.'

'What did you say your name was?'

'Virginsky.'

'That rings a bell.'

This was a dangerous moment. If Verkhotsev had talked to Ruzov about Virginsky, it would hardly have been in favourable terms. Virginsky found it hard to read Ruzov's expression. It seemed that he was deciding whether to trust Virginsky or not. Virginsky decided to pre-empt that decision. 'He probably said I was a meddling nuisance.'

Ruzov remained non-committal.

'At that time, he would have seen me as an enemy.'

'Why would he do that?'

'Because I was working for Loris-Melikov.'

'And now?'

'I am no longer, you may be assured.'

Ruzov snorted contemptuously. 'You would say that.'

'Believe me, I have seen the error of my ways.'

'How convenient.'

'No, not convenient. It was a painful lesson, in truth. I was bitten by the Wolf's Jaw.'

'Yes, that is what they call him, isn't it? Wolf's Jaw, Fox's Tail.'

'I think of a different animal when I hear his name.'

'Oh? And what's that?'

'Snake. Loris-Melikov is a cold-blooded, crawling reptile. If I must concede that he is a man, then he is a man without principles. He does not love Russia. He is not even Russian! He is a jumped-up Armenian princeling.'

Ruzov smiled in agreement. 'Admirable as these sentiments are, this is all just words. I will need more than just words.'

Virginsky slipped a hand inside his jacket and pulled out the letter that had been passed to him that night on the street outside Porfiry Petrovich's apartment building. He held it out to Ruzov.

'What's this?'

'Read it.'

As he read, Ruzov's expression slowly changed from sceptical detachment to amazement. 'This is dynamite.'

'Do you think that Loris-Melikov would consent to me handing such a letter over to the Tsar's enemies?'

'How did you get it?'

'That need not concern you. Suffice it to say that I know a man who is skilled at acquiring items that their owners do not wish him to acquire.'

'A thief, in other words?'

'There is no criminality when his acts serve the greater good.'

'And what is the greater good?'

'Need you ask?'

'I am just interested to hear it from you.'

'I have no love for the current Tsar. He has shown himself to be wicked as well as weak. I have become convinced that he does not have Russia's best interests at heart.'

'What are you prepared to do about it?'

'I am prepared to give you this letter.'

'Is that all?'

'I hope to join you, and those who share your aims.'

'Which are?'

'To hasten the day when Alexander the Second is no longer the emperor and Alexander the Third takes his place.'

Ruzov pocketed the Tsar's letter to his mistress. 'I thank you for this.'

Virginsky sensed himself dismissed. There was a slight note of panic in his next question: 'What happens now?'

Ruzov's lip curled in satisfaction. The power in their encounter had shifted in his favour. 'The letter will need to be authenticated.'

'It is genuine, you may be sure.'

'Nevertheless.'

'And then?'

'You may await our response. I will leave a message with our friend.' Ruzov nodded in the direction of the counter. 'Virginsky, did you say?'

'That's right. Pavel Pavlovich.'

'We will be in touch, Pavel Pavlovich. You may be sure of that.'

'When?'

Ruzov shrugged. 'I would leave it a week.'

Virginsky nodded as Ruzov rose from the table. The soldier picked up his copy of *Autumn Leaves* and clicked his heels.

'Oh, and what might help your... shall we say, application... do you think you would be able to lay your hands on any more of this kind of... material?'

'It's not that easy.'

'But you know a man!'

'Yes, but there's a limit to the risks I can ask him to take. I would have thought this was enough?'

'We shall see.'

Ruzov turned and strode towards the door. Virginsky watched the sword swing at his side as he went.

*

A week later, Virginsky called back at Ballet's and bought a second box of chocolates from the same saleswoman. 'Did Captain Ruzov leave something for me, by any chance? I am Virginsky.'

She turned to a shelf on the wall behind her and took down an envelope with his name on the front.

He waited until he was out of the shop before opening it. The single sheet of notepaper inside had a line of numbers neatly spaced out.

Back in his apartment that evening, he deciphered the message.

It was a laborious business flicking back and forth between the poems and counting out the letters. On the higher numbers, he counted twice just to make sure he hadn't make a mistake.

Gradually, the meaning emerged:

ANICHKOV PALACE MAY TWELVE

After that was written a time. 19:00.

May 12 was the following day.

24

Virginsky was a little early for the appointment, so he walked out onto Anichkov Bridge, lingering for a moment to admire the nearest of the four equestrian bronzes installed on each corner. Known as The Horse Tamers, the statues depicted four colossal horses being broken-in by naked men. No doubt, they were intended to illustrate the triumph of Man over Nature. But Virginsky saw something else. The powerful beasts straining against the leash had not yet been tamed. To him, Baron Klodt's magnificent sculptures symbolised those dynamic forces that human beings would never be able to harness.

He turned back just as a carriage drawn by real horses thundered past, almost mowing him down. The blur of speed sent him reeling backwards and left his heart pounding.

He quickly recovered, then waited for a gap in the traffic before trotting across to the entrance to Anichkov Palace.

Virginsky told the sentry that he was here to see Captain Ruzov. The man nodded as if he was expecting him, then pushed open the gate.

As he walked across the garden, Virginsky felt himself observed. As he reached the imposing entrance of the palace itself, the large double doors swung inwards to admit him. A pair of liveried footmen revealed themselves, gloved and bewigged like ghosts from the last century. The two men were so alike they might have been twins.

The doors closed behind Virginsky with an echoing thud.

The lackey on the right addressed him. 'Virginsky?'

'Yes.'

'Follow me.' The man turned sharply and led the way towards the back of the entrance hall. The other remained at his post by the door.

Still that sense of being watched persevered. Now it was intensified by all the portraits of Romanovs that hung on the walls. Virginsky glanced up at a severely glowering face, half-expecting to see the eyes move.

The footman led him to a white panelled door where he rapped out a complicated pattern of knocks that might have been code. He waited a moment for an answer that did not come before opening the door.

'In here.' He showed Virginsky into a high-ceilinged room, with a large table in the centre and a dozen or so chairs placed around it.

The room was empty, which made him wonder about the footman's strange knock. Perhaps it was to alert whoever had been in there to Virginsky's arrival, so that they could vacate the room. There was a door off to one side through which they could have gone. A large mirror hung on the same wall. Virginsky wondered if he was being watched through it.

Thick, brocaded drapes all the way to the floor were drawn across the windows. The lighting, Virginsky noticed, was electric. For some reason this surprised him. It seemed to go against the retrograde conservatism associated with the Anichkov Palace.

Virginsky crossed to the mirror and peered into it. It was not so much that he expected to see whoever was standing behind it, merely that he wanted them to know he knew they were there. However, once he had engaged in this little pantomime, he wondered if it were wise.

But it succeeded in provoking a response. A moment later, the door in that wall opened and a man came in.

He was aged about sixty, tall and as thin as a matchstick, with a pale, gaunt face. He wore the dry, disapproving expression of a corpse that had been brought back to life against its will. The man had the high-domed, balding head of an intellectual, though Virginsky sensed his weak chin must have been a disappointment to him. He wore small, horn-rimmed spectacles, a dark suit and bowtie.

As the man looked at Virginsky, his thin lips twitched into an expression that at first puzzled Virginsky, until he realised it was meant to be a smile.

'Thank you for coming, Pavel Pavlovich.' The man's voice was unexpectedly smooth, almost unctuous.

Virginsky bowed.

'Please.' The man gestured towards a seat.

Virginsky accepted the invitation to sit down. 'It is an honour to meet you, sir.'

The older man nodded as if he knew it was. 'You know who I am?'

'Of course. You are Ober-Prokuror Pobedonostsev.' Pobedonostsev, the arch reactionary, self-declared opponent of democracy, and ideologue of absolute power. His title of Ober-Prokuror did not refer to a judicial position. His authority was over the Holy Synod of the Orthodox Church. Pobedonostsev stood for everything Virginsky hated. And yet he must do his best to persuade this man that he was an enthusiastic supporter of his cause.

Pobedonostsev's lips twitched complacently as he took a seat across the table from Virginsky. 'First may I thank you for the material you placed in our hands. We are very grateful.' The man's strange smile froze. 'Naturally, before we can place any store by it, we need to verify the source.'

'The source?'

'Yes. How did you come by it?'

'As I told Captain Ruzov, there is a man I have used in the course of my investigations.'

'His name?'

'His name is unimportant. It could be Dmitri or Igor or Boris.' All at once, Virginsky knew who had given him the letter. 'Or Yevgeny.'

'And so… what? You commissioned this nameless fellow to steal the letter?' Pobedonostsev's tone was sceptical.

Virginsky understood why Pobedonostsev was suspicious. The letter was almost too powerful. Yes, it unlocked the door to Anichkov Palace, but its possession by a lowly state magistrate set off a clamorous alarm. Virginsky couldn't help wondering if Loris-Melikov had underestimated his opponents. 'That's not how it was. He came to me with the letter, which he had acquired in the course of his normal work.'

'His normal work?'

'I am afraid to say, he is a burglar. His normal work is

undertaken on his own account. It is only occasionally that he has put his talents at my disposal.'

'I see. And so he gave you the letter?'

'He offered to sell it to me. With men like this, nothing is given freely. Fortunately, he did not appreciate its full value. He could certainly have got more for it had he offered it to those who stand most to lose from its circulation. The Tsar's supporters. I dare say he assumed I was one of them. My larcenous friend is not a political man. He didn't know what he had here. Not exactly. He didn't understand the full significance of the letter. He thought it might be important. Explosive even, if it fell into the wrong hands. And so he brought it to me, believing that I would know what to do with it.'

'And you made sure that it did. Fall into the wrong hands.' Pobedonostsev's lips twitched appreciatively.

'Or the right hands, depending on your point of view.' Virginsky reciprocated the other man's unconvincing attempt at a smile with a grin of his own. He sensed that Pobedonostsev was halfway to believing him, mainly because he wanted to believe. 'What will you do with it?'

He saw immediately that he had overplayed his hand. The ice returned to Pobedonostsev's eyes. 'That need not concern you. You may be assured that we will put it to good use.'

'I do not doubt it.'

'There is something you must understand, my friend. If we are to go forward in this enterprise, there must be mutual trust. That is to say, you must trust us and we must feel able to trust you. As it stands, such trust has not yet been established.'

'Is not the letter itself a sign of my bona fides?'

'I rather think not.'

'But you have established its authenticity? Otherwise I would not be here?'

'Oh, the letter is genuine. I have no doubt. But are you, Pavel Pavlovich?'

'Why would I place the letter in your hands if I were not?'

Pobedonostsev widened his eyes in surprise. 'Well, I can think of one reason, but perhaps it would not be polite to mention it.'

'I would rather you were frank than polite.'

'Oh, it is only that you have been sent here as a spy.' Pobedonostsev's eyes twinkled at the notion.

'That's absurd.'

'Is it though? We had a spy amongst us. A traitor. He was reporting back to that villain Loris-Melikov. Every word we said was known to the enemy.'

'What happened to him?'

'What would you do with such a man?'

Virginsky shrugged. 'Expel him. From your circle.'

'To have Loris-Melikov send another? No. An example must be made. A message sent. *This is what will happen to all the spies you send!*'

'You killed him?'

'We made an example of him. As we will of the next spy Loris-Melikov sends. Be assured of that.'

'I am not Loris-Melikov's spy. *You* may be assured of *that*.'

'Well, you would say that, wouldn't you, my friend? But you cannot expect us to take your word for it. We must make sure of it.'

At that moment Virginsky heard a door behind him open. A moment later, everything went dark. From the touch of fabric against his face, Virginsky worked out that a bag had been placed over his head.

He fought the instinct to struggle. This was a test, he felt sure. He had to show that he trusted them and was prepared to surrender to whatever they thought necessary to do to him.

Besides, he felt strong hands grip his arms, preventing him from reaching up to remove the bag.

A cord was tightened around his neck, securing the bag in place and almost choking him. He was pushed from the chair onto the floor where he took several heavy blows to his body. He allowed himself to be kicked without resisting or attempting to shield his head.

He heard someone call out: 'Enough!'

A pain twinged in his chest. He wondered if one of his ribs was cracked from the kicking.

He felt the hands on him again. They turned him over, so that he was face down, his nose pressed into the floor.

Something sharp jabbed him in the back of the neck. His hands were pulled behind him and tied.

He tried to say something but his tongue felt as though it had swollen massively to fill his mouth. His facial muscles did not respond to his intentions. A soft, warm numbness spread all over him.

The darkness of the bag's interior merged with another darkness.

25

Virginsky opened his eyes but saw nothing. At first he thought he must be dead, but then he felt the pain in his ribs, which was now accompanied by a screaming headache. His mouth was dry and filled with a rotten taste. His arms were secured tightly behind his back.

He felt something soft against his face. So that was why he couldn't see anything. Someone had put a bag over his head. He had no real memory of it happening, just a vague intimation.

He was lying on his right side on a surface that was not completely hard, but which offered little comfort. Some kind of straw pallet, he guessed. His right arm ached from being squeezed between his torso and the board. He rolled over onto his back. The crude bed creaked beneath him. There was an answering squeak and the scurrying scratch of small claws somewhere close by.

He could hear a slow persistent dripping, echoing distantly, and just out of time with the throbbing in his head. He waited for the two clashing rhythms to synchronise. Once they were aligned, he would know what to do.

It happened just once. One drip coinciding with one fierce stab of pain. It was time to move.

He swung his body round and tried to stand. A wave of queasiness sloshed over him, forcing him down again. The back of his head struck the comfortless bed with a heavy thump.

He lay for several minutes, breathing cautiously, so as not to provoke either vertigo or pain.

The dripping and the throbbing were out of synch again.

Slowly, the details of his predicament to come back to him. At first, all he had was the general sense that something had gone wrong. But it was worse than that: the pain and the nausea and the fact that he didn't know where he was or how he had got there…

He tried to focus on what he did remember. A sentry and footmen in livery. Portraits on the walls. Some kind of palace, then. Yes, that seemed right.

Next he had spoken to a tall thin man. The conversation had not gone well. His memory of the man was hazy; for instance he could not recall his name. But he associated him with a sense of danger.

It was hard to get his mental processes in order. A tide of nausea crashed its waves repeatedly inside him. His head throbbed with a vindictive pulse. And then there was the incessant, irregular drip-drip-drip of water. Sometimes it sounded so loud that he was convinced it was dripping just by his ear. Then it would recede into the background and he almost had to strain to hear it.

His thoughts came to him through a thick fog. Images coalesced, then dissolved, each one adding a different flavour to the soup of his emotions.

A headless body lying on the ground.

A drunken merchant in a striped coat.

The watchful gaze of a policeman.

A wolf and a fox nestled together. He knew that this was unlike the other images. He had never seen it in reality. It stood for something. Or someone. And yet it seemed exceptionally vivid, more concrete than the other images, which were memories rather than a fantasy.

The ice grey eyes of an old friend, blinking comically.

The gentle smile of a beloved woman. Yes, beloved. He loved her, he realised. And the image of her smile filled him beyond words. He had to get out of here to tell her he loved her. His heart brimmed with emotion.

The tall, thin man again. He remembered something else about him now. He was wearing spectacles. But what was his name?

Suddenly, the man's name came back to him. Pobedonostsev. At the same time, he remembered his strange inability to smile.

There had been some talk of trust, he seemed to recall. Mutual trust - that was it. He had to trust them and they were obliged to trust him.

They had injected him with something. That accounted for the gaps in his memory and the hammer blow pulse in his head. Whatever it was had knocked him unconscious, and pretty quickly. Some kind of powerful narcotic then. It was loosening its grip on him gradually, allowing his mind to clarify.

How long had he been out? He had no way of knowing. More

worryingly, he wondered what he might have said while under its influence. Had he revealed the true reason he was there? But how could he, when he hardly remembered it himself?

It was something to do with the fox and the wolf. That was it! Wolf's jaw and fox's tail. Loris-Melikov had sent him.

He remembered that the matchstick man, Pobedonostsev, had referred to Loris-Melikov as *the enemy*. If he had discovered that Virginsky was working for Loris-Melikov, then there was no saying what they would do to him.

Hadn't there been some talk about making an example? But he seemed to think the example had already been made.

Was this all connected to the headless body? He felt in some way that it was, but he didn't know how. If you ever wanted to make an example of someone, that would be the way to do it.

What was the name of the man whose head had been removed? He was a soldier. A general…

He forced himself to concentrate on his mental image of the headless body. One detail came back to him. The man's signet ring bore the symbol of a rabbit. A little *krolik*…

Then it came to him. The headless man's name. General Krolikov.

So, had General Krolikov been Loris-Melikov's spy? And knowing what had happened to him, had Loris-Melikov sent Virginsky in to take his place?

The image of the wolf nestling down with the fox came back to him. A deep, visceral chill gripped him.

He realised in that instant that he could not trust Loris-Melikov and he owed him no loyalty. In fact, it was a close-run thing who he hated more: Loris-Melikov or Pobedonostsev.

His only duty was to himself. And to Maria. He had to get out of here for Maria.

He tried again to stand. This time his feet met the floor. The soles of his shoes scraped against something solid and abrasive. Stone. There was a slight echo to the sound, as if his feet were further away than they should have been. Infinitely far away, in fact. He noticed a dank smell in the air, which held a deep, penetrating chill. He could still hear the dripping water, though its location seemed to have stabilised now. It was somewhere to his left.

From these cues, he deduced that he was being kept in a cellar.

Virginsky grunted as he raised himself onto his legs, then took a few staggering steps forwards. One foot kicked against a solid obstacle and sent it clattering away from him with an empty, metallic din.

A bucket, he presumed.

A moment later, he heard the dry grind of an old seized-up lock turning, followed by the squeak of rusty hinges.

He had company.

26

Virginsky swung round to face the direction of the door, even though he still couldn't see anything. He thought he detected a delicate perfume insinuating itself into the ranker smells of the cellar.

At that moment, the hood was lifted from his head.

A young woman he didn't know, but who somehow looked familiar, was standing before him. She was wearing a housemaid's dress and apron and held a dark lantern aloft. Her face was urgent and fearful, but also exceptionally beautiful. 'Quick!' she whispered. 'You have to get out of here. They're planning to murder you.'

The maid turned and rushed away. Virginsky heard her footsteps patter on paving stones but made no move to follow her. She stopped at the foot of a flight of wooden stairs and turned back to him. 'Hurry! They *know*! They know you're a spy! They'll kill you!'

Still Virginsky held back.

'There's no time! You *have* to follow me.'

The urge to go with her was strong. She was an angel sent to rescue him. This was the only chance he had to get back to Maria. Even so, he held his ground.

The maid strode back towards him in a few brisk strides. Her face appeared flushed. When she next spoke, her voice was tinged with petulance: 'You've got to come with me! *Now!*' She even stamped her foot on the final word.

Virginsky gambled everything on the fact that he was still alive. And on her perfume. 'No.' He shook his head and smiled. 'Why should I come with you? I'm not a spy. And I'm not afraid of my friends.'

'You don't understand! They will kill you!'

'That's a chance I'm prepared to take.' Virginsky knew that if they really believed he was a spy, he would be dead already. This had to be a test.

She shook her head dismissively and hurried away up the stairs.

Yes, he had seen her before, he was sure of it now. Such beauty was not easily forgotten. He tried to remember what he had seen her in. The particular play eluded him, but he thought that it had been on the stage of the Alexandrinsky Theatre. This may well have been the best performance of her career so far. If his hands had not been tied, he would have applauded.

And then there was her scent. He was no expert in ladies' perfumes, but he would wager anything that hers was a little too refined for a housemaid's purse.

A dim light seeped down the stairs, casting a sheen over the interior of the cellar and its contents. He could just about make out the bucket he had kicked over and the straw pallet sticking out from the wall.

He walked back to the bed and sat down to wait.

*

Barely ten minutes had passed before he heard footsteps on the stairs. Captain Ruzov came in carrying an identical dark lantern to the one the actress had held. In his other hand, he brandished a long-bladed dagger.

'Stand up!' he barked.

Virginsky naturally complied.

'Turn round.'

Again, Virginsky obeyed. He felt the dagger hack away at the cord that tethered his arms.

Virginsky breathed out and rubbed his newly released wrists. He faced Ruzov with a look of mild admonishment.

'We had to make sure,' was the only defence that Ruzov offered.

'Of course. I understand. Although I confess I was a little insulted. I would have thought the letter would have been sufficient proof of my bona fides.'

'The letter could have been a trap.'

Virginsky pursed his lips as if that thought had never occurred to him. 'I suppose I should be grateful that you take such precautions. Assuming that everyone else in our circle is subjected to the same ordeal.'

'It is to be the way from now on.'

'Ah, yes. You mean in the wake of General Krolikov?'

In the dim light of the lantern, Ruzov's expression gave nothing away. Virginsky had to read everything into the slightly extended pause that came before the other man said: 'You may go now. I'll show you the way.'

'That's it?'

'We'll be in touch.'

'How?'

'Ballet's.'

Virginsky had questions but was not inclined to voice them. In fact, the vagueness of the instruction suited him. He was by no means sure that he would continue with his mission. He could simply walk away. It was not too late.

Indeed, his instinct right now was to run. He had to consciously slow his steps as he followed Captain Ruzov up the wooden stairs out of the cellar.

Ruzov escorted him through the kitchens. The cooks and kitchen maids looked up from their tasks as the two men passed, but quickly bowed their heads again as if curiosity was not for the likes of them.

From there, Virginsky was led through a labyrinth of corridors, until finally Ruzov held open a door for him. Virginsky found himself expelled onto Nevsky Prospect, into the sudden glare of sunlight and the deafening clatter of passing carriages. The door slammed to behind him.

He stood dazed, buffeted by the rush of passers-by. It was a shock to be reminded of a world where people went about their business, their lives shaped and driven by daily purpose and mundane cares.

Virginsky felt the joints of his body loosen, a physical reaction to his release.

He breathed in deeply and began to laugh.

27

As soon as he had recovered his composure, Virginsky presented himself at 2nd Rozhdestvenskaya Street station. He had no idea how long he had been held prisoner at the Anichkov Palace. Turning up for work was one way to find out.

Despite his somewhat dishevelled state, his appearance failed to provoke either reprimand or relief from those he passed. The only reaction was the quizzical flicker of a single eyebrow belonging to his clerk Zamyotov, who greeted him with a mildly irritated, 'Ah, there you are!'

From this, Virginsky surmised that he was merely a little late that morning, and had not been missing for several days, as he had feared. Alternatively, he was so dispensable that his absence was hardly noticed.

'I was unavoidably detained,' said Virginsky.

Zamyotov didn't seem interested. 'Well, the Wolf wants to see you.'

'The Wolf?' For some reason, Virginsky's mind went to Loris-Melikov.

But this was not who Zamyotov meant. 'Volkov.' The Chief Superintendent of the Rozhdestvenskaya Police District, who had been present that day in Tavrichesky Garden when General Krolikov's headless body had been found. 'There's been a development.'

'A development? In what?'

'The Krolikov case.'

'But hasn't that been closed? I mean, officially. I was told in no uncertain terms by Liputin…'

'Well, it's open again. Something has turned up. Apparently. Volkov himself insists on talking to you. Personally.'

Virginsky gave a nervous laugh. It was hardly routine for the elevated Volkov to demand attendance from Virginsky. But then this had been a particular horrific and sensitive case.

*

District Chief Inspector Volkov occupied the largest office at 2nd Rozhdestvenskaya Street station, where he sat behind the largest desk.

A portrait of the Tsar striking a commanding pose was hung on the back wall behind him. *A declaration of loyalty?* Virginsky wondered. Or a smokescreen designed to conceal Volkov's true sentiments? These days you could never be sure.

The room was imposing in scale, but shabby in its decor. The wallpaper was peeling away in places, revealing patches of crumbling plaster. Woodwork was long overdue a fresh coat of paint and a dubious stain seeped out from the centre of the ceiling. It was hard not to see it as symbolic. Behind the grandiloquent display of power, the disintegrating fabric of a doomed Empire.

Volkov looked up from the papers he was reading as Virginsky came in. His grey side whiskers, lean face, and long sharp nose gave him the wolfish look that matched his name. But today, his expression seemed haunted rather than vulpine. More like a whipped dog, than a proud leader of the pack.

A worn leather sofa against one wall tempted Virginsky with its promise of collapsed repose. But Volkov did not invite him to sit down.

'You must go to the Kunstkamera,' barked Volkov abruptly.

It was not the opening remark that Virginsky was expecting. He was at a loss to see what the Kunstkamera - otherwise known as the Museum of Anthropology and Ethnography of Tsar Peter the Great - had to do with General Krolikov's murder. 'Must I?'

'Yes.'

'May I ask why?'

'They have it.'

'They have what?'

Volkov's eyes widened in startled indignation. 'The head! They have the *head*!'

Virginsky gaped in disbelief. 'Krolikov's head?'

'Of course, Krolikov's head! Who else's? Has there been another decapitation of which I was not informed?'

'No, of course not. That is to say, not to my knowledge.'

'And so, it may reasonably assumed to be the general's head.'

'But why is it at the Kunstkamera?'

'How the devil should I know? Get over there. Ask questions. Find out who is responsible for this… outrage.'

Virginsky said nothing, still trying to process this new information.

'You had better take a policeman with you. Someone who can hold his tongue behind his teeth. We don't want this getting out.'

Virginsky nodded grimly in agreement.

111

28

Virginsky chose Sergeant Petrov to accompany him. He assumed the man was capable of keeping his tongue behind his teeth, as Volkov had put it, although he was strangely garrulous on the walk over to University Embankment. Nerves, probably. Petrov knew the purpose of their errand. It was bound to stimulate a certain unhealthy excitement.

The Kunstkamera seemed a rational enough building from the outside. It was baroque, but not excessively so.

Inside, however, was a different story.

Inside, the Kunstkamera was a vast cabinet of curiosities built around Peter the Great's original collection of 'scientific specimens'.

They enquired at the front desk for the Superintendent's office and were given a set of alarming instructions to follow: turn left at the stuffed anaconda, right at the mummified heads, and straight on past the child's leg with scorpion.

As they walked along the galleries, past the waxwork figures, deformed skeletons and totemic masks, Petrov's jaw dropped ever lower, settling at last into a fixed gape. He came to a stop completely in front of the two-headed calf, that masterpiece of the taxidermist's art.

Virginsky stuck his fingers between his teeth and whistled, as if he were calling a dog to heel. Eventually, Petrov tore himself away with an incredulous shake of his single head.

But the policeman had not progressed more than five paces when he staggered to a halt again. The breath went from him in a gasp of a horror. Virginsky sighed impatiently, before retracing his steps to see what had detained the sergeant this time. A large glass-fronted display case presented jar after jar of pickled foetuses. Virginsky craned forward to examine the forlorn, sepia-coloured exhibits through murky fluids.

Pity vied with fascination as he took in the various deformities exhibited. He was no expert on the anatomy of unborn babies, but some of these did not seem human. Perhaps they weren't? Heads gigantically enlarged, or grotesquely misshapen, or so diminished that they were hardly present. Extra limbs, missing limbs, even tails - and was that… ? No, it couldn't be! A singular horn coming out of the centre of one unfortunate's forehead.

None of these would have survived to birth, he felt sure. They may even have destroyed the mothers who bore them.

'Monsters!' gasped Petrov.

For a brief moment Virginsky was tempted to agree with him, before a more sympathetic response prevailed. 'No, not monsters. Just poor unfortunates.'

'What about their souls?'

Virginsky had to admit he was surprised by Petrov's question. But perhaps he shouldn't have been. The man was Russian, after all. 'What do you mean?'

'Is it in the jar with them or…?' Petrov looked vaguely about. 'Floating around somewhere?'

Virginsky pulled a face. 'I'm not a theologist. I'm a magistrate.'

Petrov frowned, as if he didn't quite believe Virginsky. 'You must have a view?'

'I don't believe in the survival of the soul. I'm not even sure I believe in the soul.'

Petrov looked at Virginsky as if he had just confessed to eating human flesh. 'You don't believe in the soul?'

Virginsky shrugged and gestured towards the largest of the jars. It contained a foetus that resembled an octopus with human features, its head disproportionately enlarged, its body almost non-existent apart from a set of trailing limbs. 'To me, this is simply organic material preserved in formaldehyde. The question of souls doesn't come into it.'

Petrov looked from Virginsky to the jar, as if he were trying to decide which was the greater monster.

*

At last, after several wrong turns caused by some confusion over whether shrunken heads were the same as mummified heads, they found the door they were looking for. Virginsky knocked. A muffled voice bade him enter.

The Superintendent's office was a cosy cubbyhole, fashioned out of tawny wood and brass. There were countless smaller cubbyholes within it, as well as cupboard doors and drawers that promised hidden treasures. It was impossible to take more than two steps inside, because of all the crates on the floor. The room was stuffed with mismatched objects, presumably left over from the public exhibits. At first there didn't seem to be anyone in there. Then a diminutive man in dusty clothes stepped out from behind a painted sarcophagus which stood open in one corner.

The man's face was deeply lined. Liver spots graced the dome of his mostly bald head. An unruly white fuzz stood out at the sides. The most spectacular aspect of his appearance were his eyebrows, which rose and bristled like strange, bushy antennae.

The man was stooped with age and as frail as an Egyptian papyrus. Virginsky's first thought was that he was ancient enough to be an exhibit in the museum.

The Superintendent, if this were he, regarded Virginsky through a monocle. It gave one side of his face a permanently surprised countenance, while the other side fell away in despond, perhaps as the result of a stroke.

'Who are you?' The man spoke with a thick German accent, which made it sound like he was almost choking on his words.

Virginsky introduced himself and reciprocated the question.

'I am Horst, Superintendent of Kunstkamera.'

Virginsky bowed respectfully and explained why they were there.

'At last. You.' A bony finger stabbed the air in Petrov's direction. 'Come with me.'

Horst led Petrov out through a side door. A moment later, the policeman returned holding out in front of him a large specimen jar, in which a severed head floated in preserving fluid. Although Virginsky had known full well that the purpose of their visit was to retrieve this very body part, nothing prepared him for the abruptness of its appearance.

This is not the kind of object you suddenly thrust at people, he couldn't help thinking. There should have been some veiling and unveiling of it. A cloth over the glass would have sufficed, which Virginsky could have lifted in his own time to examine what lay beneath.

But now, here it was in the room with them. Ugly and unmitigated.

The head was slightly turned in the jar so that it presented the open wound where the neck had been severed. In truth, *wound* was not a strong enough word for the obscene display. There was something so absolute about this atrocity that it demanded its own language.

The inner flesh was by now drained of blood. Strands of matter trailed in the preserving fluid, the fibres, nerves and veins that were normally held in place by the body's natural integrity. Virginsky wanted to look away, but he could not. His gaze was drawn to it with an irresistible and sickening fascination.

For a man who was not sure he believed in such things, Virginsky experienced an unsettling sensation in his soul.

To his relief, Petrov adjusted his grip on the jar, which stirred the ghastly object it contained. The head floated round into a different position. It was like watching a macabre ballet performed in a nightmare.

Now Virginsky was staring directly into General Krolikov's face - if this was indeed that gentleman's head. Krolikov's eyes and mouth were open, frozen in an expression of utter terror. A silent scream, stifled by the noxious liquid that flooded into his dead mouth and through his nostrils.

The shock of white hair that Oznobishin had mentioned wafted about in the fluid like the fine tentacles of a ghostly sea anemone.

Virginsky waited for Horst to hobble back into the room behind Petrov. 'You shouldn't have done this.' His reprimand was strangely mild if - as he seemed to be - he was accusing the Superintendent of perpetrating the decapitation. But he was not. 'You shouldn't have preserved it.'

'Too late.' Horst gave a shrug, the force of which nearly toppled him over.

'It will interfere with the medical examiner's work.'

'It is what we do here. If someone sends us a specimen, we

preserve it.'

'But surely you have never been sent a specimen like this before?'

'There was the head of Willem Mons, of course. But that was before my time.'

If so, it must have been a very long time ago indeed, thought Virginsky. He was tactful enough to keep the observation to himself. 'You must have realised that this was no ordinary exhibit?'

'It's not entirely unheard of. I remember when I was a young graduate student in Berlin...' Superintendent Horst suddenly broke off. 'But no, that was different. I am mistaken. That was nothing like this. And it was all a long time ago...'

Virginsky cut the old man off impatiently. 'When was this delivered?'

'Two days ago.'

'Why did you wait so long before notifying the police?'

'It was assumed that it was an anthropological artefact.'

'And what caused you to modify that opinion?'

'The lack of appropriate paperwork began to concern us. There had been no communication about the item. It simply appeared. We had not requested it, naturally. No one saw who delivered it. There was nothing on the packaging to indicate the sender.'

'I see. What kind of packaging was it delivered in?'

'A wooden crate, packed with straw.'

'Where is this crate now?'

'My assistant may know. I will ask him.'

'Please do.'

Horst seemed relieved to be given something to do that took him away from Virginsky's inquisitive presence. He bustled off with surprising speed.

After a few minutes, Petrov began to shake.

Virginsky regarded him with alarm. 'Do you want to put that thing down?'

'It *is* very heavy.'

Virginsky helped Petrov lower it onto the desk. Without discussing it, the two men rotated the jar so that the head was facing away from them.

'I don't see how you can carry that back to the station,' observed Virginsky.

Petrov winced at the prospect.

More time passed. Virginsky decided to occupy himself by looking round. He felt as though he were browsing a particularly eccentric bric-a-brac stall. A lot of the items appeared to be broken, as if they were awaiting repair or disposal. Fragments of pottery, dusty feather headdresses, primitive figurines and ritual dolls with missing limbs - he gazed upon them all with the same bewildered curiosity.

Finally, he pulled open a large drawer to be confronted by a confused pile of amber-coloured bones. His first impression was that they were human in origin. He gestured for Petrov to take a look.

The policeman let out an involuntary oath.

Virginsky chuckled. 'Do you think we should arrest him?'

'Who are they?'

'Somebody's ancestors. Judging by the discolouration, they are very old bones. Probably not Christians. So you needn't worry about their souls.'

As Virginsky pushed the drawer to, he heard the door opening behind him. He spun round to see Superintendent Horst come back into the room. He was struggling to hold a square packing case made out of flimsy plywood. It fell out of his hands onto the desk with a hollow thud.

The box appeared just large enough to contain the head that was floating in the jar next to it. A label on the outside read: 'HORST. KUNSTKAMERA.'

'It is addressed to you?' observed Virginsky.

'I cannot help that.'

'Do you know who might have sent it to you?'

'No!' The question clearly irritated the Superintendent.

Virginsky examined every surface of the crate, tilting it so that he could see the bottom. There was nothing else written on, or stuck to it. 'It must have been hand-delivered. Possibly by the murderer. It is a pity they were not observed.' Virginsky could not keep a note of rebuke out of his voice.

The top of the crate was loose. He lifted it off and peered inside. Sniffing dubiously, he breathed in a vaguely animal smell. 'This isn't straw,' he said.

The Superintendent answered with a bad-tempered snarl, as if he had had enough of his visitors. 'What?'

'You said the head was packed in straw. But this isn't straw. It's hay. It still has the grain attached.'

'I don't know anything about that,' said Horst impatiently. 'Now, if you have quite finished, I would appreciate it if you would take that object away.'

'There is just one more thing,' began Virginsky.

Horst's patience was clearly strained to snapping point. 'What now?'

'Do you have a trolley we may borrow? And something to cover that? We can hardly wheel a severed head along Nevsky Prospect for all to see.'

Horst muttered something in German, which though he couldn't understand it, Virginsky imagined to be unfavourable. Nevertheless, the Superintendent went off to see what could be found.

29

In a room in the Count of Oldenburg Hospital, Dr Schloss did his best to make the appalling presentable.

He removed the head from the jar and dried it with a towel, before lying it down at the top of a chromium steel table. He then placed a number of pillows in a line beneath it, before covering the whole arrangement with a sheet.

Schloss stood back to assess his handiwork, then nodded grimly to Virginsky.

'May I ask you, Doctor… the angle?' Virginsky sliced the air with one arm.

Schloss frowned for a moment before he realised what Virginsky was getting at. 'Ah, yes. It is the same. That is to say, it is the corresponding angle.'

This was the answer Virginsky had expected. It made it highly probable that the head had come from the body in Tavrichesky Garden. That is to say, it was General Krolikov's head. But soon they would know for certain. Virginsky turned to Sergeant Petrov. 'You may bring him in now.'

Petrov bowed with due solemnity and left the room.

A few moments later, General Krolikov's son-in-law, Myasnikov, came in, with Petrov trailing a few paces behind him.

Myasnikov's face was drained of colour, his lips gripped tightly together. A tremor showed in his jaw. He turned a beseeching look on Virginsky but saw no hope in the returning gaze.

It fell upon Dr Schloss to ask the absurd question: 'Ready?' How could anyone ever be ready for this?

Myasnikov drew in a sharp gasp. His head spasmed in what may have been either a nod of affirmation or a shake of refusal.

Schloss took it for the former. Besides, it was no good refusing. This was what he was here to do.

Slowly, Dr Schloss pulled down the sheet, stopping just before the awful cut-off point. Myasnikov glanced down, wincing his eyes closed almost immediately. He gave a single nod of confirmation and let out an immense and hopeless groan.

The groan built into an anguished cry. Myasnikov began to beat his chest with his fist. His eyes were squeezed tightly now, to block out the appalling vision. His legs crumpled beneath him. Virginsky and Petrov rushed to support him as they guided him out of the room.

They lowered the stricken man onto a bench in the corridor. Dr Schloss came out a moment later with a glass of water.

Virginsky watched as Myasnikov gulped it down, as to sate an unquenchable thirst. 'I am sorry I had to put you through that. But we had to be sure.'

Myasnikov wiped his lips on the cuff of his coat sleeve and cast Virginsky a recriminatory glance. His eyes were sunk in dark shadows, his face blotchy and raw in places. His hair dishevelled. He looked like he had not slept in a long time.

'I'm sorry, I don't know why I reacted like that.'

'Please.'

'You see, the absurd thing is, I hated him.' A strained smile tensed across Myasnikov's mouth. 'Everyone did. They either hated him or were terrified of him. Or both. He was a bully, you see. And…' Myasnikov broke off and shook his head. 'God knows what else.'

Virginsky waited, sensing that the man had more to say.

'It has destroyed my wife.'

'Why do you think someone would want to do this?'

Myasnikov shrugged. 'Punishment?'

'Why? What had he done?'

Myasnikov sighed wearily. 'I don't know. He was a soldier. He would say he did what had to be done. That it was his duty. But I think, sometimes, he went further than his duty.'

'You are talking about his time in the Caucasus?'

'I know nothing about that. Except… once… many years ago… I met some of his former comrades. I think they are all dead now.'

'Was there a man called Oznobishin amongst them?'

'I don't remember names.'

'What was it about them?'

'They never reminisced. They spoke only about the present. About how bad things were. Never about the past. And if ever the

120

conversation veered in that direction, they would bristle - almost in fear. There would be warning looks. Shins kicked under the table. The General would slam his fist down hard enough to make the bottles jump. It was a forbidden subject. As if there was a pact between them.'

'Did you ever find out what it concerned?'

'I had my suspicions.'

Virginsky nodded encouragingly.

'I did not like the way he looked at Danka sometimes.'

'Your daughter?'

'Yes.'

'What was it about the way he looked at her?'

'At first I thought I was imagining it. But when I told my wife, she said we must make sure that he is never left alone with Danka.' Myasnikov swallowed heavily. He looked as if he might be sick.

'Do you think that he would have molested your daughter if he had had the opportunity?'

'I think he was afraid of her. I think he might have killed her.'

'Why?'

'I don't know. My guess is that she reminded him of someone. Someone from his past. From that time. He was confused, you know. A confused old man. One had to pity him. But it is hard to pity someone you hate.'

'Why did you not tell us this before?'

Myasnikov's eyes bulged in something like astonishment as he stared at Virginsky. Then the effort of maintaining that expression became too much for him. His eyes closed. His body slumped back against the wall. 'I wanted to protect my wife. Whatever he was, he was her father. I did not want to bring that up. I had my daughter to think of too.' His eyes flickered open again and he met Virginsky's gaze. 'Besides, I am certain that he never laid a hand on Danka. We made sure of it.'

After a moment, his face flushed with colour and he flinched away from the magistrate's steady scrutiny.

30

Today Virginsky walked because he wanted to feel himself among the living once more.

But, oddly and for no reason, he felt out of step with those around him. Shoulders buffeted against his. He was repeatedly obliged to halt and redirect his step to avoid an awkward confrontation.

It was as if the living wanted nothing more to do with him.

At first he was not aware of the carriage beside him, keeping level with him as he made his way along Nevsky Prospect. Or rather, he was aware of something there, but only dimly. More interestingly, a sixth sense alerted him to the possibility that whatever it was, it was intent on him. It was interesting because Virginsky did not believe in sixth senses. He left all that to Porfiry Petrovich.

The carriage intruded on his consciousness only when the horses pulling it picked up their pace and trotted ahead of him. A door flew open and a man jumped out. Holding a workman's cloth cap on his head, he stumbled to a halt in front of Virginsky.

'You!' cried Virginsky, for the diminutive, scrawny figure blocking his way was known to him. Here was Yevgeny, the professional housebreaker who had once performed certain vital services for him. Virginsky was in no doubt now that it was Yevgeny who had slipped him the Tsar's letter to his mistress.

Yevgeny gestured towards the anonymous black carriage which had by now drawn to a halt. 'His Excellency would have a word with you.'

Virginsky peered inside where he saw a familiar figure in profile. The man remained staring straight ahead as if he believed he could not be seen by anyone outside the carriage.

Virginsky turned back to Yevgeny. 'So, you work for him now?'

Yevgeny pursed his lips, as if there was something about Virginsky's choice of words that displeased him. 'We have an arrangement, you could say. It suits us both. I am what you might call a consultant.'

'You're a thief, Yevgeny. Always have been, always will be.'

Yevgeny grinned as if Virginsky had just paid him the greatest compliment. 'Yes, but I'm an honest thief. A legitimate thief, you might say. Let me put it to you this way. I thieve, but I do it for the greater good. That's what the old man told me anyhow.'

'And you no doubt pick up a few choice items for yourself along the way?'

'There has to be a compensationary element to the arrangement. Otherwise it would not be an arrangement, but mere exploitation. I am not a man to be exploited. If you know anything about me, you know that.'

Virginsky couldn't help smiling. He realised that he had missed Yevgeny. And yes, his description of himself as an honest thief seemed just about right.

His pleasure at seeing Yevgeny was short-lived. A feeling of inescapable doom quickly settled on him as he turned to clamber into the carriage. The door was closed behind him with a click of finality. As the horses were goaded into movement, Virginsky fell into the seat opposite Count Loris-Melikov.

31

Virginsky decided to get the first blow in. 'I won't do it.'

Loris-Melikov's face opened up with wounded surprise. 'My dear fellow, I haven't asked you to do anything!'

'No, but you will.'

'I merely wished to pass onto you the Tsar's gratitude.'

'I don't want the Tsar's gratitude!'

Loris-Melikov bowed his head regretfully.

'Do you know what those people did to me?'

Loris-Melikov looked up. A glint of wonder showed in his eye. 'But the thing is, you did it! You infiltrated their circle. The mission was a success! Am I right?'

Virginsky refused to satisfy Loris-Melikov with an answer.

'You are the only man in St Petersburg, I believe, who could have pulled it off. I would go further. The only man in Russia. What you have achieved is simply astonishing!'

'They drugged me. And kidnapped me. And held me captive. They tried to trick me into betraying myself.'

Loris-Melikov smiled as Virginsky went through the various elements of his ordeal. His smile was one of admiration.

'They would have killed me if they had found out you sent me.'

'And you endured! And you prevailed!'

'General Krolikov…'

Loris-Melikov's expression became quizzical.

'He was your man, was he not?'

'What of it?'

'Is it not possible that they killed him because they found out?'

'Is that what you believe?'

'I don't know. But it's a possibility. A possibility that you must have entertained. Before you sent me in there.'

'I can see that this experience has taken its toll on you. I would not have asked you to do it, if it were not important. And as I say, the Tsar…'

'Damn the Tsar!'

Loris-Melikov appeared genuinely shocked. His voice took on a stern paternalistic tone: 'I will overlook that outburst given the ordeal that you have been through. You are a young man, venting his spleen. A certain latitude is allowed to those who have risked their lives in the service of their Tsar. And I know that you do not mean it. However, I will not tolerate a repetition of such language. Do you understand?'

The emotion welled up in Virginsky. He cuffed an absurd tear from one eye. 'You cannot ask me to go back in there.'

'*I will not.*' Loris-Melikov made this declaration categorically. But almost immediately, his tone became less absolute. 'I will not - *if* you do me the courtesy of hearing me out.'

Virginsky shook his head, in disbelief rather than refusal.

Loris-Melikov watched Virginsky closely for several moments. '*Those people*, as you call them, they would take this country back to the Dark Ages, to a time of autocracy and repression. If their agenda is allowed to succeed, everything that you have dreamed of coming to be will turn to ashes. Oh, I know that the Tsar does not go far enough or fast enough for young liberal-minded men like you. But the Tsar's way is the only way open to us at this moment. You know that. We proceed by a series of small steps towards the future that you long for. Do not do this for the Tsar. Do not do this for the Tsar's gratitude. Do it for your children. For your children's gratitude.'

'I don't have children.'

'Not yet. But one day you will. Do it for the woman you love.'

Virginsky looked at Loris-Melikov in amazement. Did the man know the secrets of his heart? 'How do you know that I love someone?'

Loris-Melikov smiled indulgently. 'One only has to look into your eyes.'

'I'm tired.'

'There is no need to give me an answer now. Think it over. When you are yourself once more, you will see things more clearly.'

'I am myself now.' Virginsky's voice was unnaturally low and calm.

The two men sat without speaking for a while, listening to the clip of the horses' hooves and the jangling of the carriage.

Suddenly, Loris-Melikov sat up, as if waking from a reverie. 'Who has the letter, by the way?'

'Pobedonostsev.'

'We must get it back,' said Loris-Melikov distractedly, as if making a mental note. 'Yevgeny will get it back.'

Virginsky smiled. It amused him to see how quickly the senior statesman had come to rely on a criminal. 'You… are not Russian, are you?'

Loris-Melikov lifted one eyebrow.

'Armenian, is that right?'

'What of it?'

'So why?'

'I'm afraid I don't…'

'Why do you serve the Russian Tsar?'

'I am a loyal subject of the Empire.'

'Don't you hate us? Once we conquered your land.'

'That is the way of Empires. Besides, I always make it a policy to be on the winning side.'

'You served in the Caucasus, did you not?'

'Naturally. It is my homeland. And so, it made sense that I should serve the Tsar's interests there. I did so faithfully for twenty years.'

'General Krolikov was there too.'

Loris-Melikov pursed his lips in a non-committal moue.

Virginsky went on: 'I believe his death may be connected to something that happened there.'

'Many things happened there. Not all reflect glory on those who were involved.'

'Did you know Krolikov at that time?'

'Our paths may have crossed.'

'That day in Tavrichesky Garden, you said nothing of this. You failed to declare any connection to the dead man.'

'I felt it best not to prejudice your investigation, confident that you would uncover whatever needed to be uncovered.'

'Did you have Krolikov killed?'

'My dear boy!'

It was not a denial, Virginsky noted.

Loris-Melikov looked at him with a wounded expression. 'You know that is not how I do things.'

'You have a hired thief working for you. Why not a hired assassin?'

'We had our differences, it's true. And the general was becoming a liability. But no, I did not order his decapitation. On the contrary, I was eager to extricate him from that assignment before he came to any harm.'

'What differences?'

'You mentioned the Caucasus. Let's just say we had divergent approaches to what may be called *the native problem*.'

'Please be more specific.'

'My method, as you know, is to win my enemies over by conciliation. I listen to what they want, then give it to them.' Loris-Melikov chuckled complacently. 'Or rather, I make them think I have given it to them. The result is the same. We are no longer enemies. But firm friends. And they will do whatever I ask them.'

'The fox's tail.'

'If you like.'

'And Krolikov's method?'

Loris-Melikov wrinkled his nose distastefully. 'He served in Circassia. During the troubles there. I heard of his exploits from time to time.'

'When was this?'

'It was the period of Russianisation.' Seeing Virginsky's blank expression, Loris-Melikov went on: '1859 to 1864. You were just a child then, I imagine?'

Virginsky nodded.

'Ah, so you will know nothing about it. Essentially, the native population had to be re-homed to make way for Russian settlers.'

'Re-homed?'

'It was decided that they should be sent to Turkey. To live among their co-religionists, where they would be better off and happier. The Turkish government supported the scheme, after certain accommodations and compensations were agreed.'

'And what did the Circassians think about this? Did they agree to it?'

Loris-Melikov shrugged, as if this was a question no one had thought to ask. 'The plan - the *order* - was only to...' Loris-Melikov hesitated as he searched for an appropriate word. 'Transport them.'

'But Krolikov?'

'Krolikov exceeded his orders.'

'In what way?'

Loris-Melikov closed his eyes briefly, before fixing Virginsky with a gaze that seemed to say: *Are you sure you want to hear this?*

He read the answer to that unasked question in Virginsky's eyes. 'That was not the first time Krolikov had been in Circassia. As a young man, back in the '30s, he was Aide de Campe to Colonel Zass. Does that name mean anything to you? No? Again, before your time, I suppose. The young have no sense of history today.' Loris-Melikov broke off to look wistfully out of the carriage window.

The count seemed to fall into a reverie. Virginsky wondered if that was all he was going to say. But then with sudden decisiveness he turned back to Virginsky and continued: 'Zass had command of the Mozdok Cossack Regiment. He was Krolikov's great hero, his mentor, you might say. When Krolikov returned with his own command thirty years later, he determined to resume the tactics that Zass had instigated.'

'Which were?'

'I heard about a certain beach on the Black Sea coast. It was where Circassian villagers were taken to await the boats that would ferry them to Turkey. Men and women of all ages, children, babes in arms. From every tribe of Circassia - Abzakh, Besleney, Bzedugh, Hatuqway, Kabardia, Ubykhia... '

'Ubykhia?' Virginsky thought he had heard the word before but couldn't remember where.

'Yes, Ubykhia is the homeland of the Ubykh, one of the twelve tribes of Circassia.' Loris-Melikov watched Virginsky expectantly. But Virginsky merely nodded for him to go on.

'Where was I?'

'On a beach in Circassia.'

'Ah yes, the beach.' Loris-Melikov paused. His expression grew distant and haunted. 'I was not there of course, but I received a report from a man who was. He described the scene most vividly.'

'What... scene?'

'Bodies. Piled up on the sand.'

'A massacre.'

'It went further than that. Krolikov's sworn aim was the total annihilation of the Circassian people. He was not the only one, of course. It became for a while unofficial Russian policy, though the Tsar himself never sanctioned it. His orders were only for the agreed deportation.'

Virginsky allowed himself to be jolted by the movement of the carriage while he absorbed all that Loris-Melikov had said. 'So Krolikov's murder may have been revenge for that?'

'Possibly. Or for one of his other crimes.'

'What other crimes?'

'One mustn't believe every rumour swirling about in time of war.'

'Tell me what you heard.'

'Rape. He is said to have instigated the use of rape as a military tactic. Regrettably, it is an effective method of cowing the native population into submission. I do not like it. I do not approve of it. I have never ordered it, officially or unofficially. I merely note that it achieves certain limited short-term objectives. So yes, commanders in the field, men like Krolikov, and Zass in his day, will countenance it, and even encourage it. It works, you see. War is a brutal business, I am afraid. But this is the price we pay for the expansion of civilisation.'

'The price *we* pay?'

Loris-Melikov corrected himself. 'The price that must be paid.'

'Did this include the rape of children?'

'Ugly rumours. But yes. I heard of that.'

'Your Tsar, the Tsar you serve, gave him licence to do that. Rewarded him for it. Honoured him.'

'The means were abhorrent. The end, desired.'

'Is that why you used Krolikov to infiltrate the Anichkov Palace faction? An abhorrent means to a desired end?'

'A man like Krolikov, with that in his past - he is precisely the

129

kind of person those retrogrades revere.'

'But how were you able to make him do your bidding?'

Loris-Melikov placed his hands together in front of his mouth, as if he were about to utter a prayer. But he said nothing.

'You used his crimes against him.'

Loris-Melikov dipped his head in acknowledgement. 'He could not bear to imagine how his daughter would look at him if she knew.'

'Is that why you kept the truth from me? To spare her feelings?'

'The truth is overrated, Pavel Pavlovich. Expediency is a better guide to action. What good is served by dredging all this up again? It was all so long ago. The world is a different place now. Circassia is Russia. That is a fact. Nobody remembers how it was achieved.'

'Somebody remembers.'

Loris-Melikov did not acknowledge Virginsky's objection. He was in full flow. 'The truth, as you call it, will only benefit Russia's enemies. It will remind the world that once we did some things that perhaps we shouldn't have. Active forgetfulness is a better policy.'

Virginsky almost admired the breath-taking cynicism of Loris-Melikov's words. But something that he said put a thought into Virginsky's head. 'That's why he was killed in such a spectacular way. To draw attention to his misdeeds. It was a performance. The killer put on a show.'

'Well, let us not indulge this flamboyant killer. Let us look the other way. And as for Krolikov, he is an unlamented man. I think we can all agree on that.'

'Are you not concerned that the killer will strike again?'

'I have the feeling, don't you, that his lust for revenge is sated. He has made his statement. My advice is that we do not give him the satisfaction of being shocked by it. We should ignore him as one would a pettish child.'

'But if he does not at first achieve the effect he is aiming for, will he not keep going until he does?'

'I see that you are determined to pursue this matter. Very well. But promise me one thing. This must never come to trial. The killer cannot be allowed his day in court. If that happens, he will put the Russian state in the dock.'

Virginsky gave no answer. Instead, he banged on the ceiling of the carriage, signalling his intention to get out.

32

That evening, as soon as he was back home in his apartment, Virginsky threw himself down onto a sofa and fell immediately asleep. He did not dream but woke up some time after midnight, suddenly wide awake and with an unpleasant taste in his mouth.

He undressed and folded his crumpled clothes and took himself to bed, but now sleep eluded him. The thought that had woken him up would not let him go. In fact, it gave rise to other thoughts.

He waited impatiently for the morning so that he could act on them.

*

At last, the next day came.

His first call was to the Kunstkamera. This time the exhibits did not detain him on his way to the Superintendent's office.

Horst greeted him with a sour expression. 'You again?'

Virginsky's question had been preying on his mind since the middle of the night. He blurted it out without any prefacing remarks. 'What was it you were going to tell us? About the one time something similar happened? In Berlin.'

Horst heaved a deep sigh. 'We were sent a number of human skulls for our collection. They were the skulls of Circassian tribesmen killed by Russian troops.'

'Who sent them to you?'

'A military fellow with an interest in anthropology.'

'What was his name?'

'Colonel Zass. I remember it because it's a German name, you see. He was one of those Baltic Germans who go into Russian military service. Besides, Zass was notorious. It was said he paid his soldiers to bring him the heads of Circassian warriors which he kept in a wax-lined box under his bed. He boiled the skulls clean and sent some of them to us for study. He believed that the Circassians were a separate species to humans, a subspecies if you will. He wanted us to prove it.'

'So this would have been in the '30s?'

'Yes, I was a young research student at the at Humboldt-Universität zu Berlin at the time.'

Virginsky nodded. 'Did you ever hear of anything like this happening in the 1860s? Under General Krolikov?'

Horst shrugged. 'If it did, no one sent me the heads.'

Virginsky frowned for a moment at the Superintendent's ironical gaze, then took his leave.

*

Virginsky's next stop was the home of his old mentor, Porfiry Petrovich. Porfiry's appearance was much improved since the last time Virginsky had called on him and his apartment had evidently been tidied. It was almost as if Virginsky's visit had been the tonic the old man needed.

Porfiry's welcome was warmer than Superintendent Horst's but he could not disguise his alarm at Virginsky's unnatural excitement.

Virginsky did not waste time with pleasantries but simply demanded: 'Do you still have it?'

Porfiry blinked out his bewilderment. 'My dear Virginsky! Do I still have what?'

'The clipping I gave you. I left it with you, I'm sure.'

'Ah yes! The article about the decapitated general. Come in, come in. I'll find it for you.'

Virginsky paced the floor impatiently as Porfiry rooted through piles of what seemed to be litter left around his apartment. At last he cried out: 'Ah, here it is! I knew I hadn't thrown it out.'

Porfiry handed the cutting to Virginsky with the news item facing up. Virginsky immediately turned it over to read the advertisement for Circus Ciniselli on the back. 'See! It is as I thought! She is the key to it all, I am sure of it!'

'Who is?'

'Lady Satanaya!'

'Who is Lady Satanaya?'

'The Ubykhian Wonder! Don't you remember, Porfiry

Petrovich? You read it out to me yourself.'

'Ah yes, perhaps I did. But still, I don't understand. Sit down, my friend. Will you take some tea? No, I fear that would be too stimulating. You are already in a state of some agitation. Tell me, what is all this about?'

'Ubykh is one of the twelve tribes of Circassia. That is to say, Lady Satanaya is Circassian!'

'And so?'

'General Krolikov was in Circassia in the 1860s, together with Oznobishin.'

'That is rather a tenuous link, my friend.'

'Except for the fact that Oznobishin's last customer before his animal feed business failed was Circus Ciniselli, where Lady Satanaya - the Ubykian Wonder - performs.'

Porfiry blinked rapidly. It was a sign that he was thinking. 'That is a slightly stronger link, I will grant you.'

'What are you doing this Saturday evening, Porfiry Petrovich?'

'This Saturday?'

'Yes.'

'Why nothing, I suppose.'

'Very well then. Would you care to accompany me to the circus?'

A childlike expression came over Porfiry Petrovich's face. His eyes opened wide in wonder. Then after a moment, a beaming smile of pure delight lit up his features.

33

They came from every direction - from north and south along the Fontanka Embankment, from the east across the Simeonovsky Bridge, down Inzhenernaya Street from the West - their faces lit by excitement, their step brisk with anticipation.

This cross-section of humanity converged on a single point, with a shared purpose: entertainment! They were the audience for this evening's performance at the Circus Ciniselli.

This was no flimsy tent, but a permanent stone-built structure as imposing as any St Petersburg palace. The circular dome which housed the auditorium bulged out behind a rectangular facade, giving it the look of an overfed temple.

Virginsky and Porfiry Petrovich joined the crowd milling impatiently in the square in front of the entrance. The three big doors were still closed. The three female statues above them beckoned teasingly, muses advertising the art they had inspired.

All at once a collective premonition seemed to grip the crowd and their disparate chatter converged into a cheer. A moment later, the doors were thrown open and the crowd rushed forwards. Virginsky and Porfiry were pulled along. Virginsky held one hand above his head, clutching firmly the two tickets that he had purchased earlier in the day.

They passed through the grand hall into the circus itself, where a female attendant in male riding habit - booted jodhpurs, red swallowtail jacket and black top hat - directed them to their seats. Above their heads, the air was ablaze with the light of countless chandaliers.

Virginsky glanced around at the other members of the audience, their eyes wide open with anticipatory wonder, big, happy grins on their faces, laughter tumbling from their garrulous lips. Everyone seemed intoxicated, if not by alcohol, then by the prospect of the spectacle that awaited them.

Then all at once the band struck up with a raucous overture that matched the crowd's mood perfectly. A dozen white horses cantered out in pairs from the performers' tunnel. All wore matching white feathers, which nodded pertly as their heads bobbed. Half of the horses had riders, members of the famous Ciniselli Brothers' troupe in their splendid red and black habits.

The audience roared their appreciation, as the troupe completed a couple of preparatory circuits of the ring. Then the tempo of the band picked up, as did the pace of the horses. The inner six - those with riders - broke away from their companions and spread out evenly around the ring. Then they executed a dazzling criss-cross manoeuvre, galloping at full pelt across each other's paths, but without colliding. It was perfectly choreographed, with the horses seemingly able to turn on a kopek.

The crowd cheered enthusiastically.

After the speed of that last movement, it was breath-taking to see the inner horses suddenly slow and execute a series of complicated dressage steps, all carried out in perfect synchronisation. The riderless horses on the outside continued circling at a steady canter.

Suddenly, one of the inner horses moved into the centre of the ring on its own, where it kicked and reared as if resisting its rider's control.

The audience gasped, enjoying their own dread.

Then the horse began to move backwards, at first walking, then building speed into the notoriously difficult backward gallop.

The crowd went wild. This horse then rejoined the inner circle, moving forwards once again, in step with its fellows.

The lead rider shouted a command and the riderless outer horses adjusted their gait, spreading out to form pairs with the other horses. Another bark of command, and the six riders raised themselves to stand on the backs of their horses, arms outstretched for balance. The riders reached one leg across so that they straddled two cantering horses. Finally, they moved over entirely to stand on the other horses. There was a rousing shout from the leader. The riders dropped down to take the saddle on their new mounts.

The riders had the typical diminutive build of jockeys. At first Virginsky had assumed that they were all men. But he now saw that this was not the case. There was one woman among them, as was clear from her facial structure and build.

The crowd applauded and whistled as the horses left the ring.

The band segued from a rousing march into a more playful scherzo. A pair of clowns emerged from the tunnel, kicking out their oversized feet, squeezing hooters, dropping into forward rolls and pratfalls. Virginsky let out a groan. He hated clowns. But he saw the delight in Porfiry's face. And the audience was laughing - at what, Virginsky couldn't fathom.

At last the tedium of the clowns' antics drew to a close and the ringmaster strode into the centre of the ring, cracking a long black whip.

His stentorious voice boomed out: 'Ladies and gentlemen, boys and girls, lords and ladies, princes and poets, welcome one, welcome all to the fabulous Circus Ciniselli! Tonight for your delight and delectation, we have assembled a show of spectacular entertainments. We began with the daring Ciniselli Brothers and their extraordinary equestrian exploits. Next you saw the world-famous Fratellini and Pais.' The audience let out a great cheer at the mention of the clowns' names. 'Yes, yes - who does not love Fratellini and Pais?' Virginsky pulled a face. 'Do you want to see them again?' Another cheer. 'I promise you, they will be back - and with their jolly friends - for more of the same japes and fun.' The ringmaster whipped the crowd up into an enthusiastic cheer. 'Now, it is my great pleasure to introduce to you our next act. Please, put your hands tumultuously together for the incredible, the beautiful, the talented, the more than talented, the wondrous, the more than wondrous, the terrifying... Lady Satanaya!'

Virginsky moved forward onto the edge of his seat. All around him the audience erupted. After a moment, their roar died down to a preternatural hush, as a thousand or more people simultaneously held their breath.

In the absolute silence, a young girl dressed in a gorgeous crimson costume walked out from the performers' entrance and took her place on the opposite side of the ring. Could this be Oznobishin's Sonya in the Kingdom of Wonder? The merchant had described the girl he saw as wearing a red bridal outfit.

A ripple of intrigued murmurs travelled round the audience.

The band began to play again. First the drum beat out a slow but steadily quickening rhythm, which was accompanied by the bass notes of a tuba. A mysterious eastern melody drifted above this sonic bed.

She came out swirling two long swords. The blades glinted brilliantly in the unearthly lights.

Lady Satanaya was dressed in a similar costume to the girl, though her bridal gown was jet black in colour. Circassian women were famed for their beauty. Even so, her face took Virginsky's breath away as much as any feat she that she might perform. Her complexion was buttermilk dusted with cinnamon freckles. High cheekbones gave her an aristocratic haughtiness, softened by a fine jawline. Her eyes, outlined in kohl, blazed with a fiery intensity, while an enigmatic smile played on her crimson lips.

Her dance was spellbinding. The swords she wielded never once ceased moving. Their motion was so fast that it seemed she was holding multiple blades in each hand. Then that illusion passed, and the swords became simply blurs of steel in the air. Her body moved in a series of emphatic poses, which gathered speed as she progressed towards the girl.

The moment came that she was standing right in front of her.

The music died away to a snare drumroll.

The swords continued to spin. Every now and then the point of one blade or the other would pass in front of the girl's face, reaching ever closer, until it seemed impossible that they would not cut her.

Not once did the little girl in crimson flinch. Her face remained placid and unreadable, right up to the moment when she dropped to her knees, a movement that was perfectly synchronised with Lady Satanaya's flashing swords. For just at that moment, the dazzling blades swept forward and sliced the air at precisely the point where the girl's neck had been a split-second before.

If there had been any slip or lapse in concentration, the girl would have been savagely cut, possibly fatally so.

Lady Satanaya let out a piercing yelp and took three paces back, before throwing first one and then the other sword high into the air. The swords continued to spin as they ascended. They seemed to hang in the air before coming back down, still spinning.

Lady Satanaya braced herself. She let out another yelp and then plunged first one hand then the other into the relentlessly whirling metal as it drew level with her. There was no break in the spinning of the swords, only now they were once again in her hands. She resumed her dance, moving backwards now.

At one point she performed a perfect somersault in the air, while keeping the swords in motion. The gasp of amazement that greeted this was so loud if filled the dome.

Lady Satanaya let out another shrill cry and then plunged the swords into the sand of the arena, one on either side of her.

The woman sank to one knee. The girl sprang forward and ran, throwing herself into Lady Satanaya's outstretched arms.

Lady Satanaya stood, with the girl clinging tightly to her. She turned slowly through 360 degrees to acknowledge the rapturous applause from all sides.

Leaving her swords to be retrieved by a stagehand she carried the girl off into the performers' tunnel.

Virginsky turned to Porfiry Petrovich, shouting to be heard over the band and the audience. 'Now!'

They pushed their way along the line of grumbling spectators. The Ciniselli Brothers had just returned to the ring with another team of horses.

34

The two men hurried back out through the now empty entrance hall into the suddenly inky night.

Virginsky's ears were ringing after the clamour of the circus show, his heart pounding with excitement. He led the way round to the performers' entrance at the rear of the dome. He scanned the street, where a line of carriages stood waiting. 'I don't think she can have come out yet. She doesn't suspect that we are onto her, so there is no call for haste on her part.'

'What will you do?' asked Porfiry.

Virginsky spied a street flower-vendor beneath a gas light on the corner. 'I shall offer her my compliments.'

'What would you have me do?'

'Stay here. Watch the stage door. If she comes out...'

'What?'

'Try to detain her.'

Porfiry nodded in acknowledgement of his instructions.

Virginsky crossed to the flower seller and bought a bouquet for a handful of kopeks. He heard Porfiry call out: 'Pavel Pavlovich.'

Turning back to his old mentor, he saw a look of concern on the other man's face.

'Be careful.' Porfiry blinked rapidly several times to emphasise his warning.

Virginsky brandished the flowers as if he believed they would be a match for Lady Satanaya's swords. In the flurried movement, one of the heads fell off.

*

Virginsky's plan nearly came undone at the first hurdle.

The stage door was guarded by a uniformed doorkeeper who was determined not to let him pass. The matter was settled, as these things usually are, by the transfer of coin. Whereupon, the doorkeeper became not just conniving but positively accommodating, even pointing Virginsky in the right direction for

Lady Satanaya's dressing room.

There was a warren of narrow corridors backstage, or to be more accurate, 'back-circus'. After a few wrong turns, Virginsky had to admit he was thoroughly lost.

A young woman in ballet shoes and the skimpy outfit of an aerialist came towards him in the corridor. She looked at the flowers and smiled. 'Ooh, are them for me, sir?'

'I was looking for Lady Satanaya.'

'That savage! Ah well, you've missed her. She's gone, and ain't never coming back, from what I hear.'

'What do you mean?'

'She's going to America. Barnum has bought her.'

'Bought her?'

'Yes, bought her and her daughter.'

'The girl is her daughter?'

'It's not right, is it? The way she swings those great swords in the poor mite's face.'

'But has she really gone? Already?'

'I saw her leaving with Barnum's agent just now. You might catch her if you hurry. But there's no future in it for you.' The girl eyed the flowers covetously. Virginsky thrust them in her hands.

Virginsky retraced his steps at a run. Turning a corner, he saw a party of three ahead of him. A smartly dressed man ushered along a figure who appeared to be a youth. The youth wore an ankle-length black coat and a top hat. He was holding hands with a young girl. Even though Virginsky could only see her from behind, he was sure it was the girl who had been wearing the crimson bridal costume, now dressed less conspicuously.

So, this was not a youth, after all, but the woman he was looking for. Of course, it was perfectly possible for a woman to put on male attire.

Virginsky called out: 'Lady Satanaya.'

Instinctively, she turned to see who called her name. At close range, her beauty was even more impressive than it had been in the ring. But there was a strange, unsettling quality to it. A detachment that made her face seem almost inhuman, more like a mask than flesh and blood. Only her eyes seemed fully alive. They flashed with a wild intensity and he saw in them the sudden realisation of why he was there and what he wanted from her. Lady Satanaya quickly pulled open her coat to reveal a long, ornately decorated scabbard. The sheathed sword was only there for an instant, but Virginsky understood the meaning of her gesture. She whispered something to the man then placed her daughter's hand in his, before darting out through the stage door.

The man stood in front of the girl, positioning himself to block Virginsky's way. He was handsome, in that square-jawed American way. A thick sandy-coloured moustache half-concealed his mouth as he spoke. His Russian was perfect, without even the hint of an accent. 'Lady Satanaya belongs to P.T. Barnum now. Any requests for an interview will have to go through me, James Bowie, Barnum's representative in Russia.'

'I am a magistrate. Virginsky. I am here on official business. I must talk to her about a very serious matter.'

'She is out of your reach now. I have the paperwork to show that she is the property of P.T. Barnum and cannot be taken by anyone without due restitution being made to Mr Barnum.'

Virginsky switched to English so that there would be no misunderstanding. 'Get out of my way or I will have you arrested!'

Bowie replied in English. 'I was merely explaining how things stand.'

He and the girl moved to one side, allowing Virginsky through.

As he emerged onto the street, Virginsky looked about hopelessly. In her long dark coat and black top hat, Lady Satanaya, it seemed, had merged with the night.

Porfiry came hurrying up to him. 'Where is she?'

Virginsky shook his head impatiently. 'Didn't you see her? She just came out of this very door.'

'That was her? The young fellow?' Porfiry pointed to the line of carriages, one of which was pulling away - a Hansom cab drawn by a single horse. 'She's in there.'

'We must stop it!' cried Virginsky.

Porfiry moved faster than Virginsky would have thought possible given his age and the depressed exhaustion he had shown not so long ago. But his involvement in the evening's enterprise seemed to have invigorated him. Without warning, the older man sprang out into the road, waving his arms in front of the oncoming horse. The carriage showed no sign of slowing down. In fact, it picked up speed. Porfiry was forced to dash to the other side of the road at the last moment.

Virginsky watched in horror as a closed carriage hurtled into view from the opposite direction.

He screamed out a warning, but too late.

Porfiry crumpled and vanished under the hooves of the galloping team. It was as if the road had opened up beneath him, so sudden was his disappearance. The driver pulled on the reins and called the horses to a halt further down the road.

There were shouts and footsteps running. Lady Satanaya's carriage continued on its way.

Virginsky ran towards the unmoving bundle of clothes lying on the ground. Blood pooled around Porfiry's head. His eyes were open, staring fixedly at the moon. As Virginsky knelt to take his friend's hand, he felt sure that the old prankster would crack a smile and turn to him, blinking his eyes for all he was worth.

But he did not.

35

The following day, Virginsky stared at the blank sheet of paper on the desk in front of him.

He was required to write a report into the death of retired magistrate Porfiry Petrovich but as yet had been unable to find any words.

He could not get past the fact that if he had not invited Porfiry along to the circus last night, his old friend would still be alive. He could blame Lady Satanaya, or her driver, or the driver of the carriage that mowed Porfiry down. He could blame Barnum's agent for delaying him at the door.

But he knew that there was only one person responsible for Porfiry's death.

Pavel Pavlovich Virginsky.

It was not just that he had taken Porfiry with him. He had urged him on to the act of folly that had cost him his life.

It was not enough to say that he had not meant for Porfiry to interpret his words in the way that he had. He had made no attempt to pull Porfiry back or restrain him.

The door to his office was closed to keep out the remorseless clamour of the station. By now, word of Porfiry's death had got round. Even those who had not worked with him directly knew of his reputation as a great investigator. The case of the student Raskolnikov was still discussed to this day. Those who knew of Virginsky's connection to the former investigating magistrate had cast pitying glances in his direction as he passed through them. In some ways that was harder to bear than the heedless chatter of those who either didn't know or didn't care.

How blissful it must have been to have awoken that morning unburdened by grief and guilt. Not that Virginsky had slept at all the previous night. Over and over he had relived the incident, trying in his mind to make the sequence of actions produce a different outcome. He had imagined himself grabbing Porfiry's wrist and pulling him back out of harm's way. How easy it would have been to have done that! How little it would have cost him!

If only he could wind back time to that moment before Porfiry sprang out in front of the oncoming carriage.

Virginsky closed his eyes in shame as his own words came back to him: 'We must stop it!'

As he mentally edited the scene, he gave himself a different script. 'Let it go!'

He imagined the look of questioning surprise that this would have provoked from Porfiry.

'It doesn't matter,' he would have explained. 'Yes, she is guilty of killing Krolikov, but he is guilty of so much more. I cannot find it in myself to blame her for what she did.' His imagined words had an artificial, speechifying ring to them. He knew that he would never have said anything like that to Porfiry in reality. Last night, it *had* mattered. Last night he had been desperate to catch her. Not because he wanted justice for General Krolikov - a man he frankly detested - but because of nothing more noble than professional vanity. Quite simply, he wanted to solve the mystery. That was the beginning and end of it. He wanted people to speak of him in the same way that they spoke of Porfiry Petrovich, as a great detective who cracked the cases others couldn't.

Besides, it would have produced the same result. Letting her go or trying to stop her. It was all the same now. Lady Satanaya was long gone. Her American protectors had made sure of that.

There was a knock at Virginsky's door. The clerk Zamyotov came in. 'I am sorry to disturb you.'

Virginsky nodded tersely. He was here, so he had to expect that the business of the place would intrude on him.

'There is a man to see you. An American.'

Virginsky sat up. He had not expected this. 'Show him in.'

James Bowie was wearing a fawn-coloured checked suit and holding a derby hat in his hands. His expression was grave and contrite. Virginsky wanted to hate the man with a fierce angry hatred but found that he could not. He was drained of all emotions other than those that pertained to his own guilt.

Bowie held out a letter. 'Lady Satanaya wanted you to have this,' he said in his immaculate Russian.

Virginsky frowned but said nothing. Neither did he take the

letter.

'She wished me to convey to you her deep regret over the death of the man last night. She did not see him jump out. If she had she would have directed her driver to stop the carriage.'

'Why can she not tell me this herself?'

'I think you know the answer to that question, and if you do not then this letter will provide it.'

'Where is she?'

'I have communicated with Mr Barnum via telegraph. He has not authorised me to provide you with that information.'

'Must I remind you, you are in Russia. Here you obey the laws of the Tsar, not P.T. Barnum.'

'Wherever I am in the world, I obey Barnum. It's written into my contract. Will you not take the letter?'

'I can arrest you for aiding and abetting a fugitive from law. A murderess.'

'Who is this murderess?'

'Lady Satanaya.'

'Please, read her letter. And then, if you still want to arrest me you will find me at the Hotel l'Angleterre.'

At last Virginsky took the letter. The American bowed, and on a releasing nod from Virginsky turned to leave. As he reached the door, Virginsky called out: 'Wait!'

Bowie looked back over his shoulder expectantly.

'I have a question,' said Virginsky.

The other man nodded.

'You speak Russian like a native?'

'My mother is Russian.'

His curiosity satisfied, Virginsky allowed the man to go.

*

Statement of Firdes Khamyta, known professionally as Lady Satanaya.

In May 1864, Circassian forces, aided by their allies the Abkhaz, made their valiant last stand against the Russian oppressors in Qbaada. After their surrender, the Circassians were driven to

THE CRIMSON CHILD

Sochi on the Black Sea coast to await boats to take them to Turkey.

The road to Sochi was lined with the corpses of women, children and elderly people who were too weak to complete the journey. They collapsed as they walked, to be set upon and eaten by wild dogs while still alive. This I saw with my own eyes, for I was one of those taken to Sochi.

I was ten years old.

I saw dead mothers still holding their lifeless babies in their arms.

But this was not the worst of it.

When we reached Sochi, the shoreline was one immense graveyard, though at least in a graveyard the dead are buried. Here the bodies lay everywhere about, with the sick and dying among them. Those starvation or disease did not take, met their ends at the hands of Russian soldiers. They wielded daggers with remorseless dexterity, staining the shore with blood.

At night, the lapping of the waves sounded like the gentle moans of the dead.

As I lay exhausted and hungry awaiting death, a Russian devil came towards me with his dagger drawn. I was too feeble to resist. My mouth was too parched even for me to cry out. I closed my eyes in expectation of the inevitable. The rest of my family was already dead. I was convinced I was about to meet them in paradise.

But that Russian devil, whose name I later learnt to be Oznobishin, had something else in mind for me.

He slung me over his shoulder and carried me to the Russian camp, where he handed me over to another man, whom I later learnt to be his commander, General Krolikov.

Krolikov had me fed and bathed, and I began to hope that there was one good Russian and this was he. But I was mistaken.

After I had recovered my strength sufficiently, Krolikov took me to his bed and raped me. When he had tired of me, he gave me to his fellow officers for them to do with as they pleased.

This torment lasted seven days, before I managed to escape. I stole a dagger from one of the Russian soldiers who had fallen into a drunken stupor. I killed him with his own blade while he lay snoring.

I slipped away in the night and ran back to Sochi to lie among the corpses. I don't know why I chose that place to escape to. Perhaps I thought they would not look for me there. Perhaps I merely wanted to be with my own people, even if they were dead. Or perhaps I hoped that the fabled boats would come and take me away. The land had once been my beloved home. Now it was a place of nightmares and death. It had been transformed into Hell, a worse-than-Hell.

Next day, a boat indeed put in and I was able to board it. I will not enumerate the horrors of the voyage. But many of my fellow passengers who had survived the journey to Sochi, now succumbed to death at sea. Their bodies were thrown overboard without ceremony or remembrance. We were a much-depleted manifest by the time we reached our destination in Turkey.

I was adopted by a Circassian family who looked after me well. I grew strong and nurtured in my heart a bitter hatred for the men who had abused me. I vowed one day to take my revenge on them. I still had the Russian's dagger, and every night I rehearsed cutting the throats of his countrymen.

At the age of fourteen I ran away from my adoptive family and joined a company of travelling circus performers. I taught myself the Circassian Sword Dance and took the stage name Lady Satanaya after the old Circassian Goddess.

When I was fifteen, I heard that Russian settlers had taken over Qbaada and renamed it Red Meadow, after the copious Circassian blood that was spilled there. My father was one of those who fell at the battle of Qbaada. His blood had soaked into the soil.

When I was seventeen, I married a Turkish acrobat and bore him a daughter, who is with me now. I loved my husband but my love for him was not as great as my hatred of my Russian tormentors. I never forgot my vow.

Last year, I left my husband and came with my daughter to St Petersburg to join the Circus Ciniselli. While I was practising with my swords one day, I saw the merchant Oznobishin arrive with a cartload of horse feed. He was much aged and gone to seed, but I recognised him as the author and originator of all my torments. My first thought was to kill him there and then but another idea came to me. I hid in the back of his cart and was thus transported back to his warehouse, where I surprised him with a dagger at his throat - the same dagger I had stolen from his comrade all those years ago.

He was a foolish and superstitious man and I made him believe that I was indeed a Goddess and that my dagger was magic.

I told him that I would kill him in his sleep unless he delivered Krolikov to me. He lied and prevaricated but eventually admitted that he was still in contact with his former commander and promised to do as I had ordered.

He ceased to deliver feed to the circus but I knew where to find him and was relentless in reminding him of his promise. As he had been a devil to me, I became a devil to him. I gave him no peace.

In time, he told me that the general would be in Tavrichesky Garden on a certain day. I went there with my sword and accomplished the fulfilment of my vow. I took my daughter with me so that she might entice the old pervert, who I knew to be feeble minded, into a secluded spot where I could kill him. She looks now very like I did when I was a child.

I packed the head in Oznobishin's hay and sent it to the Kunstkamera so that they might put it on display as the head of a genuine Russian monster, although I have no expectation that they will.

I do not recognise the so-called justice that you serve. It is Russian justice and Russian justice is founded on the blood of innocents. I am writing this only because I felt pity for the man who died, whom I am told was a friend of yours. I wanted you to understand the strange and mysterious events that led up to his death, a death I did not seek and do not celebrate.

This statement has been transcribed for me by Mr James Bowie. I speak Russian to some extent, having learnt it as a child. I am more fluent in Turkish.

The truth is I live in one language and dream in another. The language of my dreams is my mother tongue, Ubykh, but in St Petersburg there is no one who understands me when I speak it. As for my dreams, it is always the dead who speak to me in Ubykh.

I worry that one day I will forget my mother tongue entirely. The words will fly from me like ash carried off by the wind. Then when the dead speak to me, their words will mean nothing. And when I try to answer, my voice will fail me.

36

She was waiting for him when he came out, Maria Petrovna Verkhotseva. Her eyes were pink, her face puffy and drained of colour. When she saw him, she let out an anguished sob.

'Is it true?'

Virginsky nodded grimly.

'Why did you not…?' But she broke off.

'What?'

She closed her mouth tightly.

He thought he knew what she had been about to ask. 'Why didn't I come and tell you? Why did I leave it for you to read about in some horrible newspaper account? The truth is, I couldn't. I couldn't face you. It was my fault, you see. I am to blame.'

She reached out a consoling hand towards him. 'No, no, Pasha! Don't say that.'

He flinched away from her touch. 'It's true.'

Her hand fell forlornly by her side. She could no longer bear to look at him.

'So you see, I don't deserve this. I don't deserve your *Pasha*… I don't deserve your sympathy. I don't even deserve your pity.' He gave a bitter, scornful laugh, though the scorn was directed entirely at himself.

She shook her head in fierce denial. Her voice became a breathless whisper. 'My love…'

'And I certainly don't deserve *that*!'

'No! No!'

'There was a time…' He was thinking back to the period of his imprisonment in the Anichkov Palace, when he had dreamt of declaring his love to her as soon as he got out of there. He had dared to imagine some kind of future together for them both. Of course, in typical fashion, he had failed to act on his intention! Without his even realising it, his nerve had failed when he was no longer in mortal danger.

It was just as well, he saw now.

He shook his head remorselessly. 'No, I don't deserve any of that.'

They were silent now, aghast at what might happen next.

'Do you know what he said to me? One of the last things he said?'

Maria gave a minimal shake of the head.

'Be careful. He warned *me* to be careful.'

She winced at the savage irony of it.

'I'm sorry.' He lurched past her like a drunkard and began to walk. Counting his steps. Losing himself in a city that was still not his home, perhaps never would be.

Made in the USA
Coppell, TX
06 January 2024